C000104573

The

Falkenberg

Riddle

John F. Schork

The Falkenberg Riddle is a work of fiction. Any resemblance to actual persons, living or dead, business establishments, events or locales are entirely coincidental.

Copyright 2019 John Schork

All rights reserved

This book, or parts thereof, may not be reproduced in any form without permission. The scanning, uploading, and distribution of the book via the Internet or via any other means, including storage in any form of informational or retrieval system without the express written consent of the publisher, except for newspaper, magazine or other reviewers who wish to quite brief passages in connection with a review, is illegal and punishable by law. Your support of authors' rights is encouraged and appreciated.

First edition: September 2009

Prologue

Falkenberg, Germany
February 1945

A tall, powerfully built man walked across the open field toward what remained of a large wooden building. Stopping at the collapsed end of the structure he saw bullet holes in the partially burned wooden walls.

Men died here, he thought. In the distance a Horsa glider, its tail separated from the fuselage, lay in two parts. Questions flooded into his mind as he walked around the building.

A second man jogged across the field, his leather boots pushing the high grass aside.

"Comrade Colonel, the rest of the area is deserted."

"Thank you."

The Colonel knelt down and picked up a piece of wood. He held it in his hand as he surveyed the wreckage.

"What happened here, Dmitri?" he said softly to himself.

"Sir, did you say something?"

The man stood up, tossed the wood on the ground and turned away without replying.

What most people noticed first about Colonel Sergei Andreivich Volkonsky were his gray eyes. Some said they reflected a total lack of compassion. For many they realized too late they were the eyes of a killer.

An hour later those same eyes watched the trees flash past the window of a black GAZ sedan driving south toward Leipzig. Deep in thought, Volkonsky kept going over the mystery of the Falkenberg Compound. For the last three years, over one hundred scientists had lived and worked there. Near the end of 1944 the group had made a significant discovery in the process of enriching uranium to create material for a new weapon. More powerful than anything man had ever seen, this weapon might well decide the future of the world.

Two months ago a special Soviet intelligence team led by Major Dmitri Ivanov had been sent on a clandestine mission to capture those scientists. But the team had disappeared along with the scientists.

An intensive search had been conducted in all German territory now under Soviet control, but to no avail. The Americans had something to do with this, he thought. The glider is the key to this riddle.

"Slow down," he yelled at his assistant, "Stop the car."

Lieutenant Yuri Fedov slid the GAZ to a stop, dust rising from the dirt on the side of the road.

Behind a barbed wire fence Volkonsky saw a row of aircraft hangars next to an airstrip. At the far edge of the field sat another Horsa glider.

Major Dmitri Ivanov had been a protégé of Sergei Volkonsky in the Main Directorate for State Security, Special Section Four. Volkonsky

4

headed the elite group, which was the part of the NKVD responsible for the Soviet Union's most sensitive intelligence operations.

Over the last six years, Major Ivanov had become Volkonsky's agent of choice for the most difficult assignments, particularly after the German invasion in June of 1941. On mission after mission during those desperate times Ivanov had been remarkably successful. While important to the war effort, Ivanov's successes also served to advance Volkonsky's career in the secret police. Section Four dealt with only the most sensitive situations and failure could result in dismissal or in extreme cases, a bullet in the back of the head. Ivanov's superb performance had kept Volkonsky alive and in the good graces of Marshall Lavrenty Beria.

Since 1939 Beria had run the NKVD with a ruthlessness which was feared across the Soviet Union. Beria's secret police kept every aspect of the Soviet society under surveillance. Officially the Commissar General of State Security, Beria considered Section Four his own personal tool. He was a man with no conscious or scruples, willing to do whatever was required to protect himself or advance his career. History had shown that the small man from Georgian Russia did not take failure by his agents well, particularly if they were from Section Four.

As Sergei Volkonsky stared at the second glider, he knew he must find answers. To return to Moscow without an explanation for Ivanov's failure would not be tolerated by Beria. Even with an answer there was no guarantee what the consequences would be for Volkonsky or Section Four, they had failed. But where did he go from here?

Lubyanka Prison
Moscow
March 1945

Marshall Lavrenty Beria threw the flimsy message sheet on the desk in front of him and took off his glasses. A critical part of the Soviet effort to capture the German atomic technology had failed. *Stalin asks for a report and now Volkonsky says he has no answers.*

"Get me Rostov," he said into the intercom, the anger in his voice apparent to his secretary. Beria leaned back in his chair and stared out at the statute of Felix Dzerzhinsky in the square.

Konstantin Rostov's Section Seven was responsible for covert operations outside the territorial limits of the Soviet Union. Also a Georgian, Rostov had been recruited into Ministry for State Security by Beria in 1930. A talent for foreign languages and a year studying in Paris channeled the young man into foreign operations and he'd remained there ever since.

As a director, he answered only to Beria. But it also meant that he often had to take the full brunt of the Marshall's anger when covert operations had problems. His calm demeanor and youthful good looks allowed him to retain a totally passive expression during Beria's tirades. He was as confident as any man in the Main Directorate for State Security and for good reason.

Rostov knew his networks were good, very good. The growing communist movement around the world in the 1920s and 30s had been a fertile ground for recruiting potential agents. The disaffected youth of a lost generation found the stated ideals of Marx and Engels suited their sense of justice. Rostov had been very successful in cultivating deep plant agents in most of the countries of Europe and much of the

6

Americas. He had spent three years in London putting the framework together for today's very effective organization. But today his concern was how to mollify Beria's fury.

"Volkonsky thinks I can go to Stalin and tell him I have no idea what happened to our mission in Germany."

Rostov knew better than to interrupt Beria.

"We know the Americans are working on an atomic weapon. The Germans were doing the same thing. When this war is over it will be the nation which possesses these weapons that will dictate the future of the world. I know that, Stalin knows that and the Americans know it. But the cretins who work for me don't seem to understand."

"No, sir," Rostov said quietly.

"I have directed that every asset of the NKVD be mobilized to find any evidence of our men. I've sent Volkonsky personally to find out what happened. But no one has found anything. Not a shred of evidence. Worthless and incompetent!"

Rostov sat quietly waiting for Beria to continue.

"I've decided to take a different tack."

"Yes, sir."

Beria stood up and went to the window. "This is important enough to risk compromising Oscar."

Fighting the urge to object, Rostov continued to sit quietly as he pondered what Beria had just said. Oscar, a senior member of MI-5, was one of their most strategically placed undercover agents. Recruited many years ago by Rostov himself, the man was a committed communist and talented intelligence operative. Oscar had been a key member of MI-5's counter intelligence effort for over twelve years and most recently had been head of the group running turncoat German agents in England.

"Sir, I understand the criticality of this mission. I would only make the point that Oscar is our most highly placed agent in MI-5. His value in the future could be enormous."

Beria turned and glared at Rostov, his voice deadly serious. "If we don't solve this atomic problem there may not be a future for either of us. Do I make myself clear?"

Rostov realized the decision had been made. "Yes, Comrade Commissar."

Chapter One

Commander Jack Stewart, Royal Navy, DSO, DSM and DFC, turned down the corridor leading to Ward D. Only 32, he was young to be so senior. But the row of ribbons on his uniform attested to a remarkable record of service. His tanned face and rugged features made most women turn for a second look. Few people suspected that Jack Stewart commanded one of the most elite groups in MI-6.

Jack had been a regular visitor to the Ramsgate Hospital over the last six weeks. Located in the rear part of the large hospital, Ward D provided MI-6 a discrete and secure location for patients needing protection or anonymity. Guarded by Royal Marines, the wing had steel bars on the windows and extra fencing around the perimeter.

The sentry recognized him and came to attention.

9

"Good morning, Commander." The young man handed Jack the sign in sheet after examining his military identity card.

"How are you this morning, Corporal Allen?" Jack noted his time of arrival and signed his name.

"Couldn't be better, sir." The Marine walked to the door and held it open.

There were eight single rooms on the passageway. Jack knew his way to room D6 located on the right. Despite his many visits, this trip would be very different. It was time to see if his instinct had been correct. Jack knocked lightly and swung the door open.

The patient, attired in the standard blue hospital robe, sat propped up on several pillows reading a magazine.

"Good morning, Major. How are you feeling today?" Jack asked.

"Very well, Commander," he said in accented English. The powerful man shifted in bed, turning slightly to face Stewart.

Dmitri Ivanov had been near death when pulled from a collapsed building in the Falkenberg compound. The protection of another body on top of him most certainly prevented his death. Even with that grisly protection he'd been severely injured. Quick attention by an RAF physician stabilized him and allowed his transfer by aircraft to a hospital in France, then onto England. Now his features reflected a man on the mend, his face filling back out under a head of curly black hair.

Jack pulled a chair to the side of the bed and sat down. "We've honored your request that the Soviet Embassy not be made aware of the situation. I think it's time we talk about that."

"I am surprised you waited this long." Ivanov paused, trying to find the right words. "When I regained consciousness I realized my mission had failed. That operation had been personally ordered by Marshall Stalin." Ivanov paused again, closing his eyes momentarily. "He does not take failure well. Not only did I fail but your team succeeded in capturing the Falkenberg scientists. That's why I admitted my real identity to you and asked you to say nothing."

"Where do we go from here?" Jack said, deciding his strategy was playing out as planned. The Russian understood the reality he faced.

Ivanov hesitated then spoke, "I am a man without a country, Commander. I can't go home. I would be arrested and imprisoned." His voice trailed off.

"Or killed?"

"Or killed."

Jack got up and walked to the window. He trusted his instinct about men and he liked this straightforward Russian. Now was the time. "I may have an option for you."

Ivanov looked at Jack with a quizzical look.

"During our talks we never discussed politics. In fact I'm probably the most apolitical person you'll ever find. But I do believe in good and evil. And we're about to put an end to one of the most evil regimes in the history of mankind. It will be a great day for the world when we stick that bastard Hitler on the gallows." Jack walked back to Ivanov's bedside.

"What's your point?"

"Major, the world is about to change more drastically than it has in a hundred years. The United States has become the dominant world power. The Soviet Union possesses the most powerful land army on the planet. Europe's colonial powers have been devastated by this war. Asia's upside down with the Japs on the run and China waiting to take their place."

"I don't disagree. I'm still waiting for your point."

"There's going to be a struggle for power and dominance as the war winds down. I think we need to work hard to make sure mankind has a chance to come out of this with a future."

11

"One dictated by the United States and England?"

"A future that is guided by self-determination. You're no fool. A military dictatorship, whether it's German or Russian, is still a dictatorship. You admit your own future would be forfeit by that very system which operates on fear and intimidation."

Ivanov lay back and looked up at the ceiling. "I won't insult you. Most people in my country understand what it is and have no illusions. But it is the system. It's how we were raised and it's difficult to be objective."

"If the situation were reversed would you let me walk out of this hospital and go on about my business?" Jack asked.

"Is that what will really happen to me? I just walk away from here when they release me?"

"I've already said that. I guess we'll have to wait until you're released to prove it to you."

"And when will that be?"

Jack looked at Ivanov. "The staff told me you'd be ready for discharge in the near future."

Ivanov seemed surprised.

"That's what they told me yesterday," Jack said.

"Then where will I go?" The Russian asked.

"There are several places available. I'll get the staff to brief you on your choices."

"It's up to me?"

Jack laughed. "That's the way it works here."

Dmitri Ivanov sat up and turned to face Jack.

"You spoke about an option?"

Jack nodded and sat down in the chair next to Ivanov's bed.

The black Ford sedan pulled to a stop on the circular driveway leading to a large estate in the Kent countryside. Jack Stewart got out first and then turned back as Dmitri Ivanov began to exit the back seat. The Russian wore a dark blue suit with a raincoat open in front. With an assist from Stewart, he climbed out of the back seat.

"It is good to breathe fresh air," he said, surveying the grounds quickly.

A Royal Marine sentry opened the large wooden door and saluted as the two men entered.

Ivanov walked into the hallway and stopped in front of a large painting. He leaned over to read a plate on the frame. "Corry Woods, September 1931. Commander, what is this place?"

"A classic English country estate. It's called Corry Woods. The owners are in Canada for the duration." Jack looked down the hallway and saw Hiram Baker approaching. He didn't see the surprised look on Ivanov's face.

"They will come back and you'll leave?" The Russian asked Jack.

"Of course we will," he laughed. "Major, let me introduce you to one of our key officers. This is Hiram Baker. Hiram, Major Dmitri Ivanov."

The two shook hands. Baker wore standard British Army battle dress with a single crown on his epaulettes. Formerly an officer in an infantry division, he had been severely wounded in France during the German drive to Dunkirk. His gallantry under fire had been recognized by the Military Cross, however his wounds had removed him from active service with his regiment. He had been with Jack Stewart from the inception of what was now called the Double 00 Group.

"Welcome to Corry Woods, Major. I take care of the administrative details around here. Please feel free to let me know if there is anything I can do."

13

Ivanov raised his eyebrows. "Thank you."

"Jack, I've got the Major in the west wing. Follow me and I'll show you to your room."

A Royal Marine Corporal entered the main doorway carrying a small valise. "Here is your bag, sir."

Hiram took the bag and said, "This way."

The two men walked down the corridor as Baker continued, "You can rest if you'd like or look around. We'll plan on dinner at 1800. That will give you a chance to meet some of our little group."

"Thank you. You are wearing the uniform of a Major in the British Army?"

Baker turned and smiled. "Correct. I was in the infantry before joining this lot."

"And you called Commander Stewart by his first name?"

Hiram laughed. "We're a bit unconventional here. It does upset some of our more senior visitors." He stopped and opened a door. "Here's your room. You'll share the facilities at the end of the corridor."

Ivanov looked around the spacious bedroom. "Very nice."

"Is there anything you need?"

He shook his head. "No thank you. I think I will rest for now."

After 30 minutes Ivanov got up and put on his suit coat. He couldn't sleep. While he was tired, his mind kept trying to put his situation into perspective. He'd gone over it many times since Stewart outlined his proposal. While Ivanov loved his homeland, he couldn't go back and knew it. His time in the hospital and discussions with Stewart had given him much to consider. Ivanov knew what the iron fist of Stalin had done to the Russian people. As a member of the secret police he'd done many things that bothered him. But the unchecked brutality of the Red Army had made him question many things. The summary executions, intimidation and arrests committed to ensure the countries of Europe would not be able to resist the Soviet Union. Perhaps this Stewart was right, he thought. Someday Stalin would fall and he might be able to go home again. Perhaps a temporary shift in allegiance might help him to gain favor with the NKVD. But Ivanov knew he was in very dangerous territory.

He walked to the door and carefully pulled it open several inches. He expected to see one of the Marines standing guard outside the room, but the hallway was empty. Opening the door fully, he looked both directions down a deserted corridor. Grabbing his raincoat from the back of a chair he stepped into the hall and closed the door behind him.

Rather than retracing his route to the main entrance, Ivanov turned right and walked to the double doors at the end of the hallway. Peering through the window he saw a set of stairs leading down to a wide green lawn. After weeks in hospital he looked forward to fresh air and opened the door. A cool afternoon breeze greeted him and he turned up the collar of his coat. He descended the stairs with hesitation, pausing when he reached the bottom to glance around the yard. After a moment he began to walk slowly taking in every detail of the large building and grounds.

Turning a corner he saw two men in a courtyard standing next to a military truck. They were talking to one another and paid no attention to him. Continuing across the bricks of the courtyard he headed for the front of the manor. He stopped at the corner of the main building to lean against the edge of a raised flower bed. Looking south he saw a wide lawn encircled by the driveway where they had arrived.

"It's very quiet around here."

Ivanov turned to see a tall, athletic man in plain British battle dress walking toward him. The close cropped blond hair, deep blue eyes and sharp features immediately registered in his memory.

15

"I'm assuming your real name is not Haller?" the Russian asked.

"You are quite correct, Major."

The two men looked at each other. The last time Ivanov had seen this man he had professed to be a German scientist working within the Falkenberg compound. In fact he had turned out to be a British undercover agent.

"But you are German?"

"I am." He extended his hand. "My name is Karl Dietrich."

Ivanov took his hand tentatively. "Commander Stewart told me he had a diverse group at Corry Woods. I should have expected as much." Ivanov shivered, the cool wind beginning to have an effect.

"Perhaps we should go inside," Karl said.

"Yes."

Karl led him to a room off the main entrance. A small fire crackled in a stone fireplace, the flames highlighting several large bookshelves which lined the walls.

The warmth felt good to the Russian. He watched Karl walk over to a credenza and pour a drink.

"I have come to like scotch whiskey. May I pour one for you?"

"Thank you."

"Sit down. I'll bring it to you."

Ivanov lowered himself into a wide arm chair.

Karl handed him a glass.

"We call this the library although I've never seen anyone actually read any of the books."

Ivanov sipped the scotch, the fiery liquid burning his throat. "Not vodka but I think I could come to like this."

Karl sat down on the small couch.

"Am I permitted to ask questions?"

16

"Certainly."

Ivanov took another drink wondering if the German would be truthful.

"So, Karl Dietrich, how did you come to be here?"

"I was on a mission to kill a German defector."

"And who sent you to kill this man?"

"Henrich Himmler. I was a Colonel in the SS."

Ivanov's eyes flashed briefly as he raised his glass and took a drink.

"There was a German commando named Dietrich. He was credited with several assassinations of senior Soviet officers."

"I was on the Eastern Front," Karl said without emotion.

The two sat in silence.

"How did a Colonel in the SS end up working for British Intelligence?"

Dietrich stood up and walked over to the fire. He reached down and threw a small log on the coals.

"I had come to realize what the Nazis were doing to Germany. I decided if I helped stop them I might be able to live with myself."

"So they forced you to work for them?"

Karl poured another drink and held the bottle up to Dmitri who nodded.

"Not at all. Jack Stewart asked for my help with no conditions other than he thought it was the right thing to do."

This is absurd, Ivanov thought. In this business people don't ask other people to do anything because it's the right thing to do. There always has to be an angle.

"And when the war ends?" Dmitri asked.

"We'll continue working for this organization."

"You sound so sure of yourself."

Karl finished his drink. "I trust Jack Stewart."

"Can you walk away?"

"If I wanted to, but I don't. It gives me a purpose. Plus I've never done anything else. This is what I know. What would you have me do, go back to Germany and become a shopkeeper?"

Ivanov stared at the fire. What is happening here, he wondered? Is this an elaborate ruse to make me comfortable and get information? What do they want from me? Was Stewart serious when he said there might be a place here for me?

After dinner, Karl Dietrich returned to the library and saw Jack Stewart standing by the large double window.

"Gillian said you might be here."

Stewart turned and smiled. "For some reason this place helps me think."

Dietrich walked over to the bar and poured a shot of scotch in a tumbler. He held the bottle up to Stewart who nodded.

"Thinking can be a dangerous thing, my friend." He handed Stewart a glass. "To ignorant bliss," he toasted.

Jack laughed and said, "Right you are." Can it be only ten months since I met this German in the woods near here, he asked himself? A former enemy, Karl Dietrich was now a trusted friend and the best operative in the organization. It had been a remarkable war.

Karl sat down on the couch and began to massage his leg which had been severely injured on his first mission with Jack into Germany.

"Leg acting up?"

"As they say, it's the weather." Karl remembered Jack taking care of him for a week behind the lines while a group of partisans carried him to the pick up point. A relationship, which began out of necessity, had become a strong friendship between the two men.

18

"What do you think of our Soviet friend?" Jack asked.

Karl took a drink, not responding immediately.

In a moment he looked at Jack. "Let me respond with a question for you."

"All right."

"What made you bet your career and the success of that first mission on me? For all you knew I was an SS Colonel who would turn on you as soon as we got to Germany."

"Von Wollner felt your motives were genuine. Eva had known you for years and felt the same way. And I had a gut feeling about you."

Dietrich leveled his gaze at Jack. "And what does your gut tell you about our Russian?"

"I think he's one of the good ones. He knows he can't go back and there's no love lost on Stalin. I think he's a loyal Russian just like you are a true German."

Karl sat quietly and sipped on his scotch.

Jack continued, "You talked with him this afternoon. What did you think?"

"Too early to say. Are you going to offer him a job?"

Stewart walked over and sat down in a chair opposite his friend.

"If a job is offered, we'll do it in agreement. You're still the number two man around here and I respect your judgment. If you don't want Ivanov then the deal's off."

"Even though he's already seen Corry Woods and most of us?"

"We're moving out of here when the war ends and we'd ship him overseas in any case. If he tried to go back to the NKVD I doubt if he'd survive a fortnight. Particularly if we let it be known he'd helped us."

Karl nodded knowing the Soviet secret police was as brutal and unforgiving as the Gestapo.

"But we need to make a decision. The Brigadier has given me a heads up that something is coming down that's very important. He said we need to be ready for an operation in short order."

Chapter Two

Kent
April 1945

Jack Stewart thought it odd that Brigadier Noel Greene was not only driving his own car but also wearing civilian clothes. Recently retired from the Army, Greene had been the director of Section D of MI-6 when Jack joined the organization in 1942. Stewart, who had been a U.S. Navy fighter pilot, arrived in England wearing the uniform of a Royal Navy Lieutenant Commander after Churchill had struck a bargain with Franklin Roosevelt. Greene had taken Stewart under his wing in MI-6 where he had become one of the organizations most effective behind the lines operatives.

"We're almost there," Greene said as they turned onto a tree lined road." This would be Jack's first visit to Chartwell, Churchill's country home. A roadblock ahead was manned by military police. Greene slowed the car to a stop.

"No clue why we were summoned?"

"All in good time, Commander." He rolled down the window, handing his identity card to the Sergeant.

Jack reached into the inside pocket of his suit for his ID card, feeling the Walther PPK in its shoulder holster. The 00 team was required to carry their weapons at all times. Prior to an attempt on Jack's life in London most of MI-6's people took their own personnel safety rather casually. No longer.

The Sergeant checked a clipboard then handed their cards back. "Proceed, sir. I'll let them know you're here."

"There's the house," Greene said a minute later, "It's his pride and joy. The war has kept him in London or traveling so he hasn't been here much. Perhaps with the European war winding down he feels he can relax a bit."

Greene pulled the sedan to a stop in a small bricked parking area. A wide set of stone steps led up to the front door.

Wing Commander Hugh Wylie appeared in the open door and hurried down the steps to the car.

"Welcome, Brigadier. A good trip?"

"Hello, Hugh. Uneventful, that's sufficient for me." Greene said extending his hand to Wylie, Churchill's primary aide de camp.

Jack came around the car and smiled.

"Hugh, good to see you. I heard your news." The two men shook hands. Friends since Jack's arrival in England, the two men shared a common past as fighter pilots. Hugh had last flown in the Battle of Britain where he had been severely wounded.

"The medical types finally passed me for a full return to flying duties. The PM has given me my release. Two months in refresher training then out to India for a chance at the Japs."

"You don't think you'll miss all of this?" Jack said as they climbed the steps.

"Everything is becoming less war and more politics I'm afraid. When you look at the problems of peace it makes the war seem simple."

22

"A wise observation," Greene said.

They were shown into the drawing room where Prime Minister Winston Churchill sat on a wide couch. He wore a smoking jacket and had a large cigar burning in an ash tray on the coffee table. Turning when they entered the room he looked as though they had interrupted deep contemplation.

"Gentlemen, please come in," he said as he stood and shook hands with both of them.

Jack could immediately sense the serious mood. After serving as Churchill's aide during the Quebec Conference in 1943 Jack knew the great man's many moods.

"Can I offer you a glass of claret?" he asked, pouring a glass for each of them without waiting for a response.

Taking a glass from Churchill, Jack noticed Hugh Wylie had left the room.

Greene sat down in an easy chair and Jack took the opposite end of the couch.

Churchill filled his glass and returned to the couch. He picked up his cigar and took a long puff.

"I wonder if the world will ever know the true story of this monstrous war? I wonder if they will even care?"

The two visitors sipped their wine but made no reply.

"Jack do you remember when you met with the President, myself and General Donovan at Hyde Park?

Stewart recalled the meeting very well. In Franklin Roosevelt's study the two world leaders had outlined the purpose of the 00 organization.

"Quite well, sir."

"And not long after that your chaps were able to spirit those German scientists away from the Russians, exactly the type of thing Franklin and I envisioned."

"Yes, sir."

Noel Greene sat impassively. Jack could tell by the look on his face he already knew what the PM was going to say.

"Jack, we told you that 'Bishop' was our most highly placed agent in Nazi Germany."

"Yes, sir," Jack replied. He remembered the mission he had led to rescue Von Wollner from East Prussia.

Churchill paused to take a drink of his claret.

"Technically that was correct. But we have an emerging problem which concerns another senior member of the Third Reich and we need your expertise again."

The Prime Minister took a long drag on his cigar, exhaling the smoke while the two men sat in silence.

"This is a matter of the most sensitive nature. What I am about to tell you is known by only a very select group. If the true story were to come out it could affect both international relationships and the internal stability of several countries. It might even affect the alliances which we must put in place when the war is over. All of these things can be prevented if you can make your way into what is left of Germany and bring this man back to us. To complicate your task no one must ever know what happened to him. He must disappear from the face of the earth. The Brigadier can take care of the second requirement but I need you to get him out of Germany."

Jack's insides turned cold. To penetrate the shrinking Reich and get a key person out of the country without anyone's knowledge would take all the skill of his people. But the charter of the Double 00 organization was to handle the most sensitive and difficult assignments. This certainly fell in that category.

"Yes, sir."

Churchill continued, "It became very clear as the war progressed that Herr Hitler was taking greater control of the day to day management of his armed forces. His rather grandiose strategic theories were not well grounded in the realities of modern warfare. That was fortunate for us in many ways. Not only did he consistently make decisions that overrode his generals, he also accelerated the loss of men and material he couldn't easily replace."

"Bishop kept us informed of these decisions as Hitler took greater control of his military," the Brigadier added, using the code name for Erich Von Wollner. "As Hitler's Executive Assistant he could see daily evidence that the Fuhrer intended to become the world's second Napoleon."

"And the Brigadier came up with a plan that would take advantage of Hitler's assumption of total control." Churchill passed the claret bottle to Jack after topping off his own glass.

Greene continued, "I can't tell you his name but a senior diplomat of a neutral country was in our employment. We knew that he had developed a close relationship with a number of Hitler's most influential henchmen. This man felt there was one man whom we could co-opt who would have the ability to influence Hitler's future decisions."

"So we could lead Hitler to make bad decisions that would help our effort?" Jack asked.

"Precisely," Churchill said. "And now we need to get this person out of Germany."

"Was that part of the original bargain?" Jack asked.

The Prime Minister took a deep pull on his cigar before answering. "This man always played both sides, Jack. If the Germans had won the war he would have survived and prospered. Now that we are going to win he will also survive and prosper. Because we agreed to the price he asked to betray Hitler. A hell of a way to have to fight a war but to defeat that German guttersnipe I would have made a pact with the devil himself. And I am sure most of the world would describe this man as Satan incarnate."

"Couldn't we just allow him to be swept up as the war winds down and then grab him?" Jack asked.

Greene looked at Churchill who waited a moment then nodded.

"Jack, we're concerned who might capture him. There were several decisions we made that might not sit well with either the United States or the Soviet Union. Decisions made by Hitler which we influenced through our man resulted in significant losses to both of our allies. While those decisions did accelerate Germany's ultimate downfall, the strategic direction was more in keeping with our own national goals." Greene looked grim.

"One of our efforts the Brigadier is being delicate about was our attempt to get Hitler to expend his remaining reserves in a push on the western front allowing the Soviets the opportunity to decimate the remainder of Germany's Army Group East. Our strategy culminated with the German attack in the Ardennes which caught the Americans off guard."

"We knew about the Battle of the Bulge before the German attack?" Jack asked.

"Not the exact time and date but we had a good idea," Churchill said quietly.

"And if we told Eisenhower, his reaction would have tipped the Germans and they might have cancelled the attack," Greene added.

Jack said nothing. American soldiers died because of that decision. But his acceptance of allegiance to England left no room for sentimentality. To this day his unique situation had never demanded a choice of loyalties between the United States and England. Jack always knew he had to option of returning to the U.S. Navy after the war, his time in a British uniform a wartime memory. But now the two men were asking him to forever shut that door.

Churchill stood up and walked over to his desk. He put the cigar out and walked back to the coach.

"Jack, we could have sent you on this mission without telling you about the Ardennes. When you pledged your allegiance to England we did not doubt your conviction. Your words and actions have reinforced this time and again. But I am not insensitive to the moral dilemma this might present to you. If you cannot continue as before, I would understand. You know your dual commission with the United States Navy is still in effect and you can return to America." Churchill stood in front of Jack, his expression solemn.

Jack looked in the eyes of the man he had come to admire and respect over the last three years. Within Churchill he saw the spirit of a great nation, his nation now, right or wrong. "Prime Minister, I am an officer in the Royal Navy. My allegiance remains to King and country. We'll do out best to extract this man from Germany. Can you tell me who he is?"

Quietly Churchill said, "Martin Bormann, Hitler's personal secretary."

Two women and six men sat around the conference table in Jack Stewart's office. They all wore plain British Army battle dress with the exception of one of the women. Eva Papenhausen, a strikingly attractive brunette wore a pair of light wool slacks and a brown sweater.

"I'll get straight to the point. I brought Dmitri Ivanov here because I felt he could add to our group. You've had three weeks to get to know him. We're at a point where a decision needs to be made on whether or not he joins Double 00."

Karl Dietrich sat to Jack's right. To his left, Phil Hatcher, the Operations, Officer, sat with a pencil in his hand ready to take notes of the meeting. A London detective before the war, Hatcher had been with Jack from the start.

Stewart continued, "I've discussed this with all of you at some point and now I need to hear any concerns you might have. My intention is to offer Dmitri a spot in the organization barring any objections from around the table."

Captain Terry Howe, the group's Ordnance Officer, spoke up, "No issues here, Skipper. You know him better than anyone else. That's good enough for me."

Gerhard Lutjens, formally a Wermacht Captain and Karl Dietrich's partner nodded. "I agree with Terry."

Jack turned to Hiram Baker.

"I suppose I've spent as much time with him as anyone and I say yes."

"Erich?" Jack asked looking to Commander Erich Von Wollner, formerly of the Kriegsmarine and head of Hitler's Secretariat in Berlin. As "Bishop" he had been Britain's top spy in the Reichschancellery. "There's no way to know his true loyalties. However I think it's worth taking a chance. His knowledge of the Soviet secret police organization is impressive. I know we'll need that information in the future."

Hatcher looked up from his writing tablet. "I say we go with him. But we also need to keep our eyes open."

"Pam?"

Pamela Thompson sat at the opposite end of the table from Jack. An attractive young woman, she simply said, "No problems here." Her eyes met Jack's. They had talked about Ivanov. The two had known each other before the war when Jack attended Oxford. Now they were engaged to be married.

"Eva, how about you?" Papenhausen had joined Double 00 from MI-5 where she had operated for over three years as a double agent for the British.

"I saw first hand what propaganda and indoctrination can do to people before I left Germany," she replied. "My only concern is whether or not the tiger can truly change its stripes."

Karl grinned at Eva. "I did." Dietrich had been one of the most experienced commandos in the German military before he opted to switch sides during an assassination mission to England.

"But you are an exceptional individual," Eva said with a trace of sarcasm. Everyone at the table smiled. Karl and Eva had known each other in Cologne while growing up. Sent to England early in the war by German intelligence, she had offered her services to MI-5 after having learned to loathe the Nazis, agreeing to work for them only to get out of Germany. Working as a double agent she had been assigned by German intelligence to meet Karl when he came ashore on his mission to England. Their reunion had precipitated Karl's decision to switch his allegiance.

"So be it. I'll talk to Dmitri. Once that's taken care of I want to get this new operation in full gear. Erich, have you and the Admiral been able to take a look at the problem?"

Von Wollner nodded. "I was coming to brief you."

29

Later that afternoon Jack found Dmitri Ivanov in the library. The Russian sat on the couch, a book open on his lap.

"Catching up on your reading?"

Dmitri turned and smiled. "It helps my English."

Jack sat down at the other end of the couch. He had spent a great deal of time with Dmitri over the last two weeks and decided his initial impression was valid. The man's dedication to Russia was strong but he had no loyalty to Stalin or the Communist government.

"Now that you've had some time to get to know our little group, what do you think?"

"They seem very dedicated to each other."

"They've been together for several years and gone through some difficult missions. That has developed a tight bond among them."

"Which brings me to the question of where I fit into this?"

Jack paused then said, "We'd like to you become an active member of our group."

The Russian's eyes narrowed and he closed the book.

"What exactly does that mean?"

"You would become part of the team, contributing your knowledge and experience to whatever task we are assigned."

Dmitri had thought about this a great length. "I would be considered an equal member of the team, not an outsider who is only let in on what is "safe?"

"Just like every other member of the team. We don't have a first and second team. If you don't believe me you'll just have to try it out and see for yourself."

"And if I say no?" Dmitri's expression showed he understood the potential he might not survive if he didn't join the team.

"I won't try and fool you. You've seen a lot here and that's not something we want to share with your former employers. We would send you to the United States while letting the NKVD know you were alive and cooperating with us. You've already said returning to Russia would be dangerous. We would ensure that."

Dmitri smiled slightly. "A good plan. You would guarantee a death sentence for me if I tried to go home."

"Not something I want to do, I assure you." Jack knew this was a critical point.

"But if I throw in with you I will be able to operate much as I choose?"

Jack nodded.

"And what would prevent me from jumping ship at some point?" Dmitri asked.

"Nothing really. But if we're good judges of character you won't. I'm willing to take that bet, as is the rest of our little band. Your addition to the group was unanimous."

Dmitri paused as Jack's statement sank in. "Dietrich told me how you trusted him based only on instinct. I guess I found that hard to believe. Now you are ready to do the same for me."

"Dmitri, if we don't ever put our trust in people, what's the point of doing what we do?"

The Russian sat on the couch and realized what held this group together. He knew he wanted to be part of that.

The two men sat silently for a moment.

"Jack, I would be proud to join your group."

They stood and shook hands.

Chapter Three

Leipzig
April 1945

Following a month of investigations, interviews, and interrogations, Sergei Volkonsky had finally pieced together a probable scenario for what occurred at the Falkenberg compound. The lack of bodies, live or otherwise, led him to conclude that the team members were either dead or prisoners of the group that landed in the Horsa gliders. Witnesses noted a great deal of air activity in the area on the 5th of January. There were also landings at the small airfield by aircraft that matched photos of Dakota transports. It seemed logical the scientists were transported on those aircraft. But what about our team? Volkonsky knew Beria wanted an answer. Unfortunately he didn't have one to offer.

"Comrade Colonel, we may have had some luck."

The Colonel looked up to see Yuri Fedov standing in the door.

"What do you have?"

The Lieutenant walked across the room and handed a single sheet of paper to Volkonsky.

"The 42nd Military Police Battalion responded to our request for any information on the German soldiers which Major Ivanov used on his team. All the names came up empty except for one, a Sergeant Werner Ruess."

Colonel Volkonsky scanned the paper as his assistant continued.

"They processed a prisoner by that name near Kamenz. The man was consigned to the main prisoner holding area in Rothenburg. They assume he's still there."

"Get me a map."

One hour later the two men left for Rothenburg.

Once Major Szenitchev, commander of the prisoner holding facility, saw Volkonsky's identity card he could not have been more cooperative. Fear of the NKVD ran deep in the Red Army.

Thirty minutes later Volkonsky sat in a small office with a large pot of tea and hard crusty bread on the desk in front of him. There was a knock at the door.

"Come."

The door opened slightly. "Sir, it's Major Szenitchev. I have the prisoner."

"Bring him in."

Two guards, both carrying machine pistols, escorted a tall man wearing a dirty German uniform into the room. His hands were bound with rope.

"Release his hands and leave us," he ordered.

While one guard untied his hands the man eyed Volkonsky warily.

"We will be outside, Comrade Colonel," the Major said as he left the room and closed the door.

"Sit down," Volkonsky ordered in German.

The man complied.

The Colonel had been around military men most of his adult life and felt he was a good judge of character. This man appeared calm. Perhaps he has given up hope.

"What's your name?" he asked.

"Ruess. Sergeant Werner Ruess."

Volkonsky stared hard at the man. The Sergeant returned the look without flinching.

"Are you the same Werner Ruess who was part of a team led by a Major Ivanov?"

Sergeant Ruess looked surprised but said nothing.

"Well?"

A look of resignation came over the man's face. "Yes......sir."

"And you took part in a mission to Falkenberg, Germany?"

Ruess nodded.

"Sergeant, I assume that your countrymen are not aware that you spent almost a year in the service of the Soviet Union working for Major Ivanov.

Ruess shook his head.

"No, I thought not." The Colonel sat back in his chair. "I suspect you wouldn't survive long if that information was released."

"No, sir," the Sergeant said quietly, looking down at his clasped hands.

"I need information," Volkonsky said.

Werner Ruess looked up.

"I want to know what happened at Falkenberg. Do you know that?"

"Yes, sir. I was there," Ruess said, his voice more forceful.

"Tell me everything you can remember."

The Sergeant talked for twenty minutes detailing the events of that day in January.

"You saw Major Ivanov carried from the remains of that building?"

"Yes, sir."

"And you are sure he was alive?"

The man nodded. "He was on a stretcher. The British put him on one of the trucks heading for the airfield."

Volkonsky got out of his chair and began to pace.

"This force that landed in the glider, you are sure they were British?"

Ruess nodded.

Finally I have something to send to Beria. It was the British, not the Americans.

"You're coming with me, Sergeant. If you can continue to provide information that is useful you will not only survive but prosper. However if you try to play games with me I will kill you. Are we clear?"

The Sergeant's eyes opened in the realization of how his life had just changed. "Yes, sir."

Rear Admiral Walter Kaltenbach removed his reading glasses and sighed. "Jack, this is going to be very difficult."

"Admiral, I didn't expect it to be anything else. But with your connections to the network I hoped something would open up," Jack responded.

Kaltenbach had been the number two man in German Naval Intelligence when Jack and Karl Dietrich convinced him to defect to England and join their group. Unknown to them at the time, the Admiral belonged to a group of senior officers in the German intelligence services. Known simply as 'the network' this group worked to preserve Germany in the aftermath of a war they all knew was lost. Despite his defection the Admiral remained an active member of the network. Distinctions between sides were beginning to blur as Europe threw off the German yoke to the Soviet and Allied forces. His counterparts in Germany continued to provide intelligence to Kaltenbach as they desperately tried to protect Germany from the Soviet onslaught. Now the Admiral saw this connection as key to their success.

"I didn't say it couldn't be done. I said it would be difficult. Everything we know right now places Bormann in Berlin with Hitler. I'm confident this information is accurate. But the ultimate destination of either man will be difficult to determine. At one point there was a discussion of the National Redoubt, a fall back position in Bavaria near Berchtesgaden. However that was also based on having forces available to man the defensive areas that surrounded the mountain retreats."

Jack walked over to a large wall map of Germany.

"Is this an accurate estimate of the current Russian advance?"

"Hiram updated it this morning based on messages from SHAEF Headquarters. I suspect they're as accurate as anything at this point."

"So if our target is in Berlin, he's surrounded by Russian forces."

The Admiral nodded. "The only way in or out now is by aircraft. They are running a steady stream of light aircraft in after darkness. So it is still very much within their capability to move individuals out of the city."

Jack shook his head. Bormann could fly out at any time to unknown destinations.

"We need to get someone in there as soon as possible to put a tail on him. That's assuming we can find him."

"Jack, if he's there he'll be at Hitler's side. That will be in the bunker under the Reich's Chancellery."

"I've never been to the bunker but I know of it." Karl Dietrich sat across the desk from Jack, maps of Germany and Berlin scattered between the two men.

He continued, "There are offices and living space for the inner circle. Himmler's adjutant and I talked about options for Himmler in the event the fortunes of war turned on Germany. Although Himmler wasn't happy with the idea of being in Berlin."

"I can't think anyone would want to be there now with the amount of bombing that's still going on."

"Aerial photos I've seen don't show much left to bomb. The city is in ruins."

"That makes me think Bormann would be in the bunker if he's still in Berlin."

"A good assumption," Karl said.

"So how do we get someone in there to find Herr Bormann and who's that person going to be?"

Karl stood up and walked to the window. A former Colonel in the SS, Karl knew he was the best person for the job. He had actually met Martin Bormann in 1942 and would know him on sight. In addition he understood the SS security procedures that would be in place protecting Hitler. Like Jack he also knew the dangers of returning to an embattled Berlin with the Red Army poised to crush the capital. But for Karl the additional danger of an immediate death warrant hung over him after his defection. If he were recognized the mission would be over and he would be dead.

"I should go. I know the city and the SS. If we can get some kind of support at that end, I could fly in and try and find Bormann."

Jack didn't respond. He knew Karl was right. In the last two years Karl had survived two missions into Germany. Sending his people into danger was the most difficult thing Jack had to do, but it came with the job.

"I agree. Although I wish there was another way. Why don't you and the Admiral see what options we have. Let's get together later tonight and make some preliminary decisions.
This thing is unrolling a lot faster than I expected so we need to get busy."

Karl found the Admiral in his office, several folders open on his desk.

"Come in, Karl, I expected you."

He sat down opposite the older man whom he had known for almost eight years. The two had developed a strong friendship before and during the war, their personalities very similar.

"If I can fly into Berlin and find out what this situation is, that would give us the best chance of finding Bormann and getting him out. The critical issue would be support in Germany."

Kaltenbach nodded. "I agree in principal. But providing a contact and support will be very difficult. As the Red Army closes in on Berlin it will only get harder."

The two men sat quietly, both grappling with the challenge before them.

"There are still two army groups facing the Russians, Army Group Vistula and Army Group Central," Kaltenbach said, thinking aloud.

Karl looked up from his own thoughts. "Any contacts there?"

The Admiral sat back in his chair and ran his hand back over his short gray hair. "There is a possibility. Although it's one I don't want to use. This man has already done more than most. But he's also in a unique position to provide the kind of support we need."

"Who are we talking about?"

"The plot to kill Hitler involved a small number of actual conspirators. Most of them have been tortured and executed, although a very small number have survived. One of them is a member of the network. He's also the Chief of Staff of Army Group Vistula."

Chapter Four

London
April 5, 1945

A brilliant blue sky greeted Londoners on their way to work, the sign of an early spring. Spirits were upbeat in the city as the war in Europe staggered to its now inevitable end. Phillip Kent did not share the joy of his countrymen as he sat in the back seat of the government sedan making its way to his office at MI-5. Currently the director of the counter-espionage section, Kent knew that the deadly game he had been playing for years just became more lethal.

Recruited as a young graduate student at Cambridge, Phillip Kent joined the intelligence service in 1931. Through hard work and a little patronage he had risen to a directorship earlier than his peers. The war solidified his position within MI-5 as the agency expanded exponentially to handle the German threat to England. But Kent worked for two masters and now a message from deep in Russia threatened to destroy his ordered world. Staring out the window, Kent was lost in thought trying to decide how he could accomplish the instructions from Moscow. Would this mission compromise his identity and send him to the Soviet Union for the rest of his life? Could he elude his own people from MI-5 if he had to flee England? Although he knew the possibility had always existed, it had remained in the background until yesterday.

Briefed on the disappearance of the Falkenberg scientists he had been told to be alert for any information that might locate them. His discrete efforts yielded nothing and he had decided it was a dead issue. A second message which arrived yesterday pointed him in a direction that could spell disaster if he wasn't very careful and extremely lucky. The message said an NKVD officer had located a German prisoner who had been at Falkenberg. The soldier told this officer it was a British operation. He was later able to identify one of the British officers from surveillance photos taken by the Soviet Embassy. That officer was Commander Jack Stewart of MI-6.

While there was cooperation between the different intelligence organizations, close familiarization was not the rule. Kent happened to know Noel Greene and had worked with MI-6 on a combined action early in 1943 involving Eva Papenhausen. At Greene's request Eva had been transferred to MI-6 but still remained officially part of MI-5. There had been a smattering of reports back from Greene on activities of the section. But a clear division remained between the two agencies.

If MI-6 had been involved in the Falkenberg mission perhaps he could get information out of Eva, at least enough to satisfy Moscow. But would Greene let him near her and what information could or would she provide?

"Phillip, do come in," Noel Greene said as he warmly grasped Kent's hand. "It's been entirely too long. I was delighted when my secretary said you had rung."

"We're all too busy for our own good, my friend." Kent took the seat that Greene waved him toward.

"I think a drink is in order. What can I fix you?" Greene stood in front of a small row of glass decanters and turned to look over his shoulder.

"Anything very old would be fine."

Greene poured two stiff measures of brandy, handing one to Kent.

"Now tell me how you've been. It seems like an eternity since we talked."

Phillip Kent spent a few minutes on some of the more interesting activities of his group that he was able to share. While it sounded very spontaneous, Kent had scripted this part of their meeting as soon as the appointment was set.

"We anticipate an increased level of activity within the department when the war ends. So much to do and too few to do it."

Greene nodded. "We're seeing the same thing. For the last five years we normally knew the identity of friends and enemies. I suspect the new world will make that infinitely more complex."

Kent nodded in agreement as he took a sip of brandy. "I think maintaining a sufficient level of experience among our operatives is going to be a challenge. We're finding many of our people are opting for a return to private life. That's one of the reasons I wanted to talk with you."

"Why do I feel there's a fox in my henhouse?"

"Noel, you were always one step ahead of me." Kent smiled. "Actually I was hoping to see if I could entice Eva Papenhausen back

42

into the fold. She's one of the best field agents I've ever seen. I wanted to appeal to her sense of loyalty."

Greene said nothing in response.

"Noel, we're all in the same situation. I would just like to talk with her about an opportunity in my group. And even though she's still officially on the roles of MI-5, I would never dream of not getting your blessing first."

"I'll tell you what. Talk with Eva. If she wants to return to MI-5 it's her decision. However if she decides to remain with us, you'll allow her move to become permanent."

"Fair enough. By the way is Jack Stewart still running the section?"

Greene nodded. "He's put together a very talented group. Glad they're on our side."

"I'd like to talk to her as soon as possible. I'm headed for Harwich the day after tomorrow. I could stop and see her on my way." Kent stood up.

"Splendid but don't forget our bargain."

The door clicked closed and Noel Greene sat back in his chair his hands interlocked in his lap. His cheerful demeanor now replaced with a grim stare. A minute later he leaned forward, picked up the telephone and dialed a number.

"Something's up. Can you break away and come in to London?"

I've been assured we'll have a Junkers 34 ready for us within a week in Dortmund. The Allied front lines are about 200 miles from Berlin, well within the range of the Junkers." Karl had circled Dortmund on the map that lay spread on the desk.

"You still think going in as an SS officer is the best idea?" Jack asked.

"No one is going to cross a senior SS officer except the Gestapo. And I suspect with Germany coming apart, you won't find many of those bastards still on the job."

Jack said, "You'll need someone to cover your back."

Karl turned to look at his friend. "Your German is very good but not perfect. It could make the difference."

"I'm willing to risk it," Jack said, knowing Karl would try to talk him out of going on the mission.

"Are you trying to be a hero?" Karl asked. "Don't you think it would be better to be back here running things?"

"Hatcher is more than capable of coordinating back here. In any case you and I have more experience than anyone else. I don't think this is a single man mission."

Karl hesitated for a moment then said, "All right but make sure Pam knows it was your idea."

"And Eva thinks it was my idea to send you?"

"Of course, I don't need her angry with me!"

The two friends laughed.

"How about flying the Junkers?"

"Thought I'd call Tangmere and talk with Dicky. They should have someone who can fly a crate like that."

Karl turned serious. "I'm not worried about the flying part of it. But landing at night in strange terrain going to take a hell of a pilot."

Phillip Kent waited in the main hallway of Corry Woods. He heard footsteps coming from the stone hallway and turned to see Hiram Baker.

"Mr. Kent, good to see you. My name is Baker."

"Yes, Major, I remember you. It's been a while."

"Quite so. I have a runner going to get Eva. She's out on the pistol range. Shouldn't be more than five minutes."

"Thank you. Sorry for the inconvenience but I do need to talk with her."

"No problem, sir. We didn't know exactly when you might arrive or we'd have had her available straight away. If you'll follow me, you can wait in the library."

Baker opened the door and Kent followed.

As the two men entered, Dmitri Ivanov stood up from the couch, a book in his hands.

"Dmitri," Hiram said, acting surprised the Russian was in the room.

"I was working on my English. Jack and Karl weren't ready for me yet," Dmitri said.

Hiram stood to one side as Ivanov and Kent came face to face.

"Phillip Kent, may I present Dmitri Ivanov."

The two men shook hands, Kent staring intently at Dmitri.

"A pleasure to meet you," Kent said, working hard to keep his voice steady.

Hiram spoke up as the two men looked at each other, "Mr. Kent has worked with us in the past, Dmitri. We learned very early in the war that breaking down the walls between the departments was the only way we could beat the Nazis."

Dmitri smiled. "I'm afraid that lesson still needs to be learned by the Soviet government. Perhaps some day." He tucked the book under his arm and said, "Please excuse me, I'm sure you have business to discuss."

Eva entered the library and looked with surprise at Phillip Kent.

45

"Hello, Eva."

"If you two will excuse me," Hiram said and left the room, closing the door behind him.

"Phillip, I never expected to see you at Corry Woods."

"Eva, please sit down."

Kent took the chair opposite the couch.

"You look well. Country life must agree with you." He smiled at her as he sat back in the chair, crossing his legs in the manner of a man totally in control.

Eva said nothing, her eyes showing uncertainty.

"The war in Europe will be over soon. And that means that we in the government will go back to subsistence funding. The battle between Germany and England pales in comparison to interdepartmental battle for funds." He smiled at his own humor. "My job is to make sure that MI-5 comes out on top." His voice now had a hard tone to it.

"Phillip, what does that have to do with me?"

He looked hard at her. "You're going to help me."

"Why would…." She stopped in mid-sentence, knowing why she would do what Phillip Kent told her to do.

"Exactly, my dear."

Chapter Five

In the distance he could hear the muffled crump of artillery, now a constant companion to the retreating German Army. His watch told him it was 0430 but time had become something that had lost relevance. In his heart he knew the final bloody climax of the war was not far off, but he still did his duty. He had always done his duty.

Major General Albert Haselman, Chief of Staff, Army Group Vistula sat on a wooden bench reading an intelligence summary which had just arrived. A man who was always careful of his appearance, his unshaved face and red eyes told the story of an army on its last legs. During a retreat of over 2000 kilometers, the strength and heart of a once proud army had been left littered in the fields and forests of Eastern Europe. Pursued by two Russian Army Groups, these veterans of three years of some of the most savage fighting the world had ever seen now had their backs against the wall – Berlin.

He rubbed his eyes and tried to focus on the paper. His thoughts kept returning to the fundamental question of how this army could continue to fight with no fuel, ammunition or replacements. Many of the front line combat units were reporting only 30-40% effective strength. He remembered the heady days of 1942 when this same army had crushed the Red Army, sometimes rolling over 100 kilometers in a day. Now they had less than that distance to Germany's capital and little to throw against Marshall Zhukov's army group.

"Would you like some coffee, Herr General?"

He looked up to see his orderly, Sergeant Dieter Hoffman. The General had gotten used to the bitter coffee substitute made from ground walnut shells. At least it would be hot.

"Thank you, yes."

The big man turned and left the tent, a look of concern on his face. Hoffman had taken care of the General since the fall of 1939. He had been one of the original members of the 21st Panzer Division, which Albert Haselman had taken command of in 1938.

Dieter Hoffman had reported to the 21st division directly from the advanced armor training course. Injured in an accident, he would have normally been released from active service. However a chance encounter when the General was visiting the hospital had resulted in Hoffman being assigned as his orderly. Over the years the two men had developed a mutual respect and friendship. Now Hoffman worried the constant strain of responsibility was destroying his General.

Albert Haselman had been an infantry officer during the first war, seeing action against the Russians then the British. Able to remain as part of the small post-war German Army he had realized the future potential of the tank and became a champion of Germany's armor build up. His enthusiasm was also shared by the man who would later command the German armored thrust into France, Erwin Rommel. The two were close friends and relied on each other as the war dragged out. When Rommel had mysteriously died in October of 1944, Haselman thought he would be next. Both had been quietly supporting the group that had made an unsuccessful attempt on Hitler's life. Everyday the General expected a visit from the Gestapo but knew there was nowhere to run.

"Sir, Major Franken is here. He says it's very important," Hoffman said as he placed a steaming mug on the table.

Hearing that name the General's focus returned instantly. "Have him come in. Sergeant please bring another cup of coffee."

Klaus Franken entered and stood briefly at attention, nodding his head. "I am sorry for arriving at this hour, Herr General. It is something most urgent."

"Please sit down, Major," Haselman said, knowing that Franken wouldn't be here unless something was very wrong. "You came from Berlin?"

Franken's eyes showed a fear that the General had never seen before. Had they been discovered?

"Yes, sir."

"How are the roads?"

"The only safe time is at night. Russian fighters seem to be on the prowl any other time."

Haselman thought of the once mighty Luftwaffe, Goering's pride and joy. Now the air force that had ruled Europe was reduced to a skeleton force with no fuel and fewer pilots.

"And what would make you run the Russian gauntlet?"

Franken reached inside his tunic and withdrew a piece of paper, handing it to the General.

It was deathly quiet in the tent, the artillery in the distance now still.

"My God," the General said after reading the paper.

"Do we have any of that cognac left, Sergeant?" The General sat staring at the table and didn't look up at his orderly.

"Yes, sir." Hoffman was surprised. Albert Haselman never took a drink during the day and the sun had just come up. "Would you like more coffee also?"

Haselman shook his head. "Pour one for yourself. I don't want to drink alone."

In a moment the big man returned carrying two glasses. He placed one on the table and sat down on a large packing box next to the desk.

"Have you heard from your wife?" the General asked.

"Not for over a month."

The sound of bursting artillery rumbled across the tent, the impacts very close. Haselman seemed not to notice.

"Soon you shall go home and see her."

Hoffman took a drink then said, "Is it almost over?"

The General nodded.

"There are over two million men of the Red Army on the other side of the Oder. We have less than 600,000 to oppose them. All we can do now is try to delay the Russians long enough to let as many of our people as possible escape to the Americans and British."

Another salvo of artillery burst nearby, the Sergeant flinching as the concussion rolled over them.

"I need you to go to Berlin."

"Sir?"

"Find my son and bring him to me."

Dieter Hoffman knew Major Wilhelm Haselman well. The young man had served as his father's aide during the heavy fighting of 1942. Severely wounded during an enemy strafing attack, he was now physically disqualified from combat. Major Haselman worked at the Chancellery in Berlin as a member of Hitler's military staff.

"What shall I tell him, Herr General?"

Haselman sat quietly for a moment then said, "Give this to him, he'll understand." He handed a coin to the Sergeant.

The constant hum of ventilator fans seemed to give life to the stark concrete walls of the Fuhrerbunker. An artificially lit world buried under six feet of reinforced concrete, it now provided protection for the small inner circle of Adolph Hitler. Driven underground by the day and night attacks of Allied air forces, the leader of the German Reich had withdrawn into a fantasy world where everyone tried to maintain an appearance of normalcy.

The senior staff understood the inevitable end they faced as Germany's armed forces fell back on every front. The inner circle had no illusions as to their ultimate fate but continued to conduct business as if this phase of the war was simply a minor inconvenience. The visitors from the hell that existed outside the wall were struck by the seeming disregard by the bunker inhabitants for what was actually happening to Germany.

"Herr Major, there is a Sergeant who is asking for you at security post twelve."

Wilhelm Haselman, the head of Hitler's radio communication staff, looked up from a message he was reading. An imposing figure, Haselman had been a star athlete at the University of Munich. Joining the Wermacht after graduation in 1937, he had followed his father into

51

the Panzer Corps. Wounded in Russia, he was now limited to staff duty, his right arm almost useless at his side.

"Did he identify himself, Sergeant," he asked the SS security man.

"I'm sorry, sir. Sergeant Dieter Hoffman," the man replied, his eyes remaining fixed on the far wall.

"Have him escorted down. I will meet him in the communication center."

Haselman looked forward to seeing Hoffman. He'd know him for many years and after serving as his father's aide, he felt that the Sergeant was more of a friend than subordinate.

Dieter Hoffman had been lucky to escape any significant delays as he made his way through roads choked with troops moving forward and refugees that were fleeing the Russians. Carrying a travel order signed by the Chief of Staff, Army Group Vistula, the Sergeant also cleared the security checkpoints that had been set up to catch deserters.

The orderly's dirty uniform and unshaven face were in stark contrast to the impeccably turned out SS escort who showed him into Haselman's small office off the main radio room.

"Sergeant, it is good to see you," he said, extending his left hand.

Hoffman smiled wearily. "You are looking well, sir."

"Here, sit down and I'll get you some coffee – real coffee."

Something in Hoffman's eyes told Willy Haselman that things were not right with his father. He leaned behind the big Sergeant and swung the door closed.

"How is my father?"

The Sergeant nodded as he sipped the hot coffee.

"Tired, but well. I'm not sure when he sleeps anymore. The artillery never seems to stop."

Hoffman put down his coffee and reached into his breast pocket. "Your father told me to give you this."

Willy took the coin from Hoffman and examined it. A five Reichsmark coin from 1935 with the image of Hindenburg on one side and the Imperial Eagle on the reverse told him everything he needed to know.

"How did you get here?"

"I have a truck and driver outside."

The trip back to General Haselman's headquarters had taken almost twelve hours. Air raid warnings caused delays and several times they had to leave the highway to bypass bomb damage from the marauding Soviet fighter bombers. But Willy Haselman knew after seeing the coin that it made no difference, he must see his father.

Artillery rumbled in the distance as they pulled into the grove of trees that served as a camouflaged vehicle park for the headquarters. Stepping out of the truck Willy saw the reflections of the bombardment against the dark eastern sky. Clustered around a small trailer, a dozen field tents housed what remained of the staff. Soviet air attacks had taken their toll of the men whose job it was to direct three German armies in the defense of the Reich. Lanterns were already being lit by the soldiers as Dieter Hoffman led Willy to a tent next to the trailer.

Pushing the flap open his left hand, Willy ducked his head and stepped into the dimly lit interior.

Albert Haselman looked up from a map he was studying and saw his son. Without a word the General stood up and came around to meet Willy. The two men embraced.

53

"Thank God you're alright."

"Father, I'm fine. But what about your message?"

The older man motioned to his son to sit.

"I don't know how long we'll be able to delay the Russians. We know they're massing for a major thrust across the Oder. Once across the river, they could drive to Berlin in two days."

Willy laughed ironically. "You'd never know that in the Fuehrerbunker. It's business as usual."

"They are fools, they have destroyed Germany." The General rubbed his eyes, the fatigue obvious to his son. "If only Von Stauffenberg had succeeded."

"Why did you send me the coin?" Willy asked.

"It seems we have one last duty."

Willy thought his father's remark sounded odd, almost like a final statement before dying.

"While you were aware of our small group, you didn't know I was part of a larger organization. We call it the 'network.' A group of senior officers has been trying to do what we can to preserve and protect Germany in defeat. We know the Russians will exact a terrible revenge. It's conceivable they'll try to destroy Germany forever, like the Romans did to Carthage."

Willy said nothing. The fatigue on his father's face faded as he continued.

"I've fought the Russians and the British. I may not like either of them but I respect the British. They fight for what they believe and they are honorable. The Russians are animals. They would gladly destroy their own people to achieve their goals." The words came fast and the tone was harsh. "We can't let them crush Germany when the war is over!"

The General reached behind him for a bottle. Putting two coffee mugs in front of them he poured cognac into both. Holding the cups up he looked at his son and said, "To Germany."

"Germany," Willy replied.

The two men sat in the silence, artillery rumbling again in the distance.

"The network has been slowly establishing relationships with the British and the Americans. Right now we have commanders on the western front who are actively helping the Allied ground campaign. The goal is to do everything we can to hurt the Russians."

"How can we do that?"

"Many ways. Our entire intelligence network, agents, files all can be given to the West. They'll use it to counter the Russians after the war."

Willy sat back and tried to take in everything his father had said. He knew these were times that would shape history and now he realized how drastically.

"And to these ends, I'll ask you to do something no father should ever have to ask his son. What we have to do is straight forward, but dangerous. If we succeed we may help save Germany." Albert Haselman looked at his son, both of them knowing that failure likely meant death.

Chapter Six

RAF Tangmere
April 1945

Squadron Leader Dicky Thompson walked across the neatly kept lawn to the brick operations building. Carrying his flying gear in one hand, his other hand held a cigarette. Taking one last puff he threw the butt on the ground, stepped on it and went into the building.

"Squadron Leader, Group Captain Toms would like to see you."

Sergeant Adair handed Thompson a mug of tea.

"Right now?"

"He said as soon as you returned."

"Right," he said turning around and heading down the hall to Tom's office.

"You wanted to see me, sir"

Toms was standing by the large window watching a Spitfire Mark IX on final. He turned and walked to his desk.

"Interesting phone call from your friend Jack Stewart."

Dicky and Jack had been friends from their days at Oxford.

"I haven't talked to Jack in several weeks, any problem?"

"They wanted to see if we could handle an insertion flight using a captured German aircraft."

Dicky put his cup down on the desk.

"Really? They do come up with some of the strangest requests."

"Assuming the aircraft is materially sound," Toms said, "It shouldn't be a problem."

"Do we know what they're looking at?" Dicky asked.

"A Junkers 34, twin engine, very much like our Hudson."

Thompson had logged many hours in the dependable Hudson bomber which 161 squadron used to support behind the line operations on the continent.

"Where's the aircraft now?"

Toms pointed to a spot on the large wall map.

"At the civilian airport in Dortmund."

"Then we could fly in a maintenance crew to check and service the aircraft."

"I think our first task is to make sure it's even flyable," Toms said.

"Are we officially tasked?"

Toms nodded. "Right after Stewart called I got a call from Group, who had been contacted by Fighter Command. I guess the word came right from the PM's office. So let's get on with it."

"So we're going to try and fly into what's left of Germany in a borrowed aircraft."

"Precisely," Toms said flatly.

"I better get up to see Jack and find out everything we can."

"Agreed. In the interim let's get the wrench turners on their way to Germany. We'll see if the kite will actually fly."

The next morning a Hudson bomber left the airfield enroute Dortmund. Aboard the aircraft were four of 161 squadron's top mechanics along with several cases of aircraft hardware and servicing material.

"Here are the coordinates that came in from our contact." The Admiral placed a pin on the large wall map.

"How confident are we that the front lines will remain in place long enough to pull this off?" Karl sat back, rubbing his eyes.

Jack stood up and stretched his back, the planning session now in its second hour. "Too hard to call."

"Then we need to carry a portable radio," Karl said, the other two men nodding in agreement.

"There's another issue. With the German defenses crumbling we might very well have to deal with our Soviet allies," Kaltenbach said.

"Why am I thinking that's something we need to avoid?" Karl laughed.

"Quite right, I'm afraid. Perhaps we can load the deck in our favor," Jack said.

The other two men looked at him.

"Is it time to call on our newest colleague?"

Karl started to say something then held himself.

Jack continued, "Think about it. If Dmitri is with us and we end up with our backs against a wall, we can let him take the lead. Either he talks his way out of any jam or we put on some charade using his NKVD credentials."

While the idea seemed far fetched, the Admiral and Karl had learned to reject nothing without thorough analysis. And the most improbable course of action had often proved to be the most successful.

"Well there's certainly room on the Junkers. We could give him the same disguise that he used at Falkenberg."

There was a knock on the door.

"Come in," Jack said.

"Sir, there's a Squadron Leader Thompson here to see you."

"I believe our chauffeur has arrived."

"So we have a set of coordinates of where we think we're going, but don't know for sure?" Dicky asked.

"I think you can plan on not landing at an airfield unless it's one of those outlying strips we've been hearing about. The Luftwaffe has been dispersing what they have left of their fighters to small grass fields around Berlin."

"And we know where they are?" Karl asked.

Dicky nodded. "Many of them. But few are lit and so we would have to get in during daylight."

Jack and Karl looked at each other.

"It all depends what we hear from the network," Admiral Kaltenbach said.

"But we don't know when that will be," Jack added.

"So standby to standby, right?" Dicky grinned at them.

"Right." Jack replied as he threw a magazine at his friend.

Jack Stewart had always been an early riser. During flight training he would volunteer for the early flights knowing the winds were lighter and his instructors still fresh. The habit had proved beneficial in every assignment during his career. Now he sat in his office, the clock indicating 0550 as he sipped his second cup of coffee. Reviewing maps and photographs of Berlin, he was memorizing the area they would be operating in during the mission.

"Jack, you need to see this," Hiram Baker said, walking into the office.

"A little early for you isn't it?" Jack asked. Seeing the look on Baker's face he knew something was wrong.

"They called me from the comm center," he said and handed Jack a single piece of paper.

"To all commands, all theaters. White House announced late today that President Roosevelt has died of a cerebral hemorrhage. The death occurred this afternoon at Warm Springs, Ga. Funeral services will be held Saturday afternoon in the East Room of the White House. Interment will be at Hyde Park Sunday afternoon. No detailed arrangements or exact times have been decided upon as yet."

Jack stared at the paper, the news hard to comprehend. The President, who had led the country out of the Great Depression and orchestrated the soon to be victory over the Nazi's was gone. He felt empty, almost as if fate had cheated both the man and the country. Jack remembered his first meeting in the Oval Office when the President had sent him to England 1942. FDR's charm and force of personality had made a lasting impression on the young Lieutenant. Two years later he'd been called across the Atlantic to meet with Roosevelt and Churchill at Hyde Park to lay the groundwork for the new Double 00 organization. Again he felt Roosevelt's strength of purpose. Now that was forever gone.

"I'm sorry, Jack. I know how you felt about him."

"He was one of the greats, Hiram," Jack said. "At least we still have Churchill."

Chapter Seven

The Fuhrerbunker
April 1945

Martin Bormann sat in his small office quietly reading through a stack of papers. Despite the imminent collapse of the Reich government, Bormann found himself compelled to continue his administrative duties as the head of the Party Chancellery and Secretary to Adolph Hitler. Over the last three years that diligence and his loyalty to Hitler had made him the second most powerful man in Germany. Himmler, Goebbels and Goering had come to detest and fear this quiet and efficient administrator. His control of access to Adolph Hitler had made him the true power behind the throne. Now that was all to end.

Bormann had read the intelligence estimates from his best agents as German forces fell back on both fronts. It was no longer possible to halt the inevitable. But Bormann, always the loyal assistant, continued to maintain the fantasy world that Adolph Hitler had build around himself. That world included a host of imaginary forces that were now converging on Berlin to turn the tide of battle. Much like the theatre, everyone in the bunker had a role to play while awaiting the final curtain.

Adolph Hitler had given direction to Martin Bormann's life. In the turmoil of the post-war upheaval, the Fuhrer was a leader whom he could follow. While Bormann's original enthusiasm for National Socialism had stemmed from his bitterness over the first war, he was not a rabid fanatic. He understood where the power would lie and made sure he was part of it. But now reality was screaming at him to abandon a hopeless situation and find a way out. Something would turn up he was sure. Martin Bormann was a survivor and the end of the Third Reich would not be the end of his story.

He looked up as Else Krüger entered. His secretary looked tired, the constant strain of living in this artificial world taking its toll.

"Herr Mueller is here to see you. Shall I show him in?"

Bormann detested Heinz Mueller, a security agent who worked under the control and protection of one of his bitterest rivals, Heinrich Himmler.

Maintaining an impassive expression Bormann watched Mueller enter.

"I am busy, Herr Mueller, what do you want?"

Mueller flushed, Bormann's tone, coupled with his disregard of Mueller's rank of SS Standartenfuhrer were both indications of the senior man's lack of respect for the former policeman.

"Herr Minister, Reichsfuhrer Himmler has asked me to intensify my efforts to ensure the Fuhrer is fully protected."

Bormann sat back, the man's arrogance trying his patience.

"And you don't think the Fuhrer's SS bodyguard is capable of protecting him from behind 30 feet of concrete?" Bormann's voice was tinged with sarcasm.

"Sir, it is not the threat from the outside I fear. Just as in the July plot it is the treachery and treason of those close to Adolph Hitler that likely pose the greatest threat."

"And what would you have me do, Herr Mueller?"

"Sir, I am sharing this with you under the instructions of Reichsfuhrer Himmler. We'll be conducting a thorough investigation of everyone to detect anything out of the ordinary. Your assistance is critical to the success of our investigation."

Bormann stared at the man. "Do what you will. Now leave me, I have work to do."

The younger man's eyes flashed with his hatred of Bormann but his voice was professional and solicitous. "As you wish, Herr Minister."

Bormann stared at the door in thought. While he didn't fear Mueller, he was concerned that the meddlesome man could complicate his plans for escaping the certain death sentence of remaining in the bunker. It was only a matter of time until the Red Army overwhelmed the city. He had no illusions of what that army would do to the survivors of the battle. The brutality of the Germans during their invasion of Russia had been duplicated as the Red Army fought its way west. Now the inhabitants of Berlin would suffer for three years of cruelty by the Wermacht on the Eastern Front. Martin Bormann had no intention of paying that price.

Willy Haselman closed the communication log on his desk. Each shift supervisor in the communication center maintained a record of important messages and any action taken during their watch. Normally Willy gave the log his full attention making sure that nothing had been missed during the night watch. But this morning his mind kept returning to the meeting with his father. Closer than many fathers and sons, the two men had developed a mutual respect and admiration for the other. Their time in combat against the Red Army had only cemented the relationship, both men watching the other rise to the challenge and danger that modern warfare brought to a soldier's life. But now he knew that his father was not only working against Hitler but with the British. Didn't that make them traitors to Germany? There was a difference between removing a monstrous dictator and actively helping the enemy. He massaged his right arm, the pain always with him, a constant reminder of that day in Russia when he had become a cripple.

His thoughts shifted to the task before him. Contact Martin Bormann and pass on the plan to rescue him from Berlin. It was crazy, he thought. One of the most powerful men in the Third Reich, Bormann was Hitler's friend and personal secretary. This man was working with the British also? The last three days seemed like a nightmare to the young Major. He'd sworn an oath of loyalty to Adolph Hitler. His father had always told him that nothing was more important to an officer than personal honor and loyalty. Now he had to make a decision.

Willy stood in front of the desk as Martin Bormann read the single piece of typed paper. He watched as Bormann placed the paper flat on the desk in front of himself.

"This is marvelous news, Herr Major." Bormann's round face broke into a smile.

"Yes, sir."

"Who else knows of this?"

"Only yourself and the Communication Shift Supervisor, sir."

"I will tell the Fuhrer. Give me one hour then release the message to all."

Willy turned to leave.

"Herr Major," Bormann said as he stood up. "Have you heard from your father lately?"

He was aware that his father and Bormann knew each other but did his question mean something else?

"Yes, sir. Just recently."

Bormann looked him in the eye. "And how is he?" he asked, his tone totally noncommittal.

"As well as I could hope, Herr Minister."

"Quite so, these are trying times for all."

"Yes, sir."

"Trying times that require decisive action to prevent disaster," Bormann said. "Wouldn't you agree, Herr Major?"

"Yes, sir." Willy turned and left the office. Did Bormann know something? He thought back to the conversation with his father.

"There will be a British team coming in by aircraft. Their job is to get Bormann back to a rendezvous point where he will be flown out. I knew their only real hope for success would have to involve you. Without someone inside the bunker, chances of success are minimal. Even with your knowledge it will be difficult to get Bormann away."

Still stunned at his father's admission of complicity with the British, Willy had only told the General that he would standby for any future messages. Did Bormann know of the rescue plan from another source?

His father had told him that once the time of the team's arrival was known he would contact him. Whatever happens must take place soon, he thought, the Russians won't wait much longer. Still torn by his loyalty oath, Wily returned to his office deep in thought.

Chapter Eight

Corry Woods

April 1945

"Early morning landing on the 16th," Jack read from a message. "The landing area is in a large open area located three kilometers southwest of Seelow. There are three lakes bordering the area on the south and west."

Jack had just returned from London when the message arrived from the network.

"Time will be short," he said to Karl and Hiram.

"We've arranged air transport leaving from Tangmere in about six hours," Hiram said. "So we need to have you on the road no later than 1300."

"The uniforms and papers should arrive anytime for the three of us," Karl added.

"Have you talked to Dmitri?" Jack asked Karl.

He nodded.

"How about the ladies?"

"Not yet."

Jack handed the message to Hiram. "I'm going to find Pam. See if you can get an update on the uniforms."

"I'll call right now."

"And you, my German friend, need to talk to Eva."

Dietrich sighed. "I know."

"When do you leave?" Pam asked. She sat at the small table by the window in Jack's bedroom.

"1300, then air transport from Tangmere to Dortmund courtesy of the RAF. Dicky will be waiting at that end." He finished shaving and dried his face on the small hand towel.

Pam got up and came over to him, slipping her arms around his waist.

Jack turned and put his arms around her. "I know. You don't have to say it."

"It just seems that you've done your share," she said, still holding him.

"That's not the point. Karl and I have the best chance of pulling this off. It's important and so we go. Its as simple as that."

Pam released him, crossing the room and sitting down next to the small case open on the bed.

"How long?"

"I wish I knew. Our contact will help get us into Berlin and locate the target."

"And you still can't tell me who it is?"

Despite Pam's security clearance and knowledge of MI-6, Jack had been told that only a small group could know the target was Martin Bormann. "No. The fewer people that know the better. Trust me." Jack knew that he was now playing on a different level in the intelligence game. If Bormann was to disappear with the immense knowledge he had of the Nazi regime, who knew what other events were taking place. The lines of right and wrong that were so clear during the war had begun to blur. All he could do was execute the orders of his Prime Minister and not worry about the morality.

Pam turned to look out the window. She hated the Nazis and the war. Last year she lost her father to a V-1 and now the man she loved was going back into the battle. It seemed like they had always been at war and it would never end.

"Karl, are you mad?" Eva asked, her expression a mix of bewilderment and anger.

"No I'm not mad. Jack feels, and I agree, that the two of us have the best chance of success on this mission. What would you have me do, send Gerhard or Terry?"

"Why not?" she asked, her voice sharp.

"Because it's my responsibility."

"God save us from the righteous soldier doing his duty," she said, turning away from him and walking out the door.

Karl had nothing else to offer her. He understood her frustration but he also knew that Jack was going into Berlin. His best chance of getting back out was with Karl at his side. That was the way it had to be.

After the cleanliness and organization of RAF Tangmere, the airport at Dortmund resembled a junkyard. In the late afternoon sunlight many of the buildings showed damage from allied bombings and the recent battle for the city. Two partially destroyed fighters, their fuselages burned and blackened, were the only evidence of the former Luftwaffe presence. On the perimeter Jack could see several British tanks, a clear indication of who had captured the city.

"Right on time," Dicky yelled up from the tarmac as Jack, Karl and Dmitri climbed down from the Hudson. Jack turned up the collar on his coat as a cold wind whipped across the concrete.

The men shook hands as Jack introduced Dmitri to Dicky.

Two jeeps were parked by the tail and the four men walked to them as two soldiers loaded several bags into the second jeep.

"Check your gear to make sure everything's here," Dicky warned.

A quick survey showed that the uniforms, radio and weapons were all accounted for and stowed in the second jeep.

"All set," Jack said and climbed into the jeep beside Dicky. Karl and Dmitri climbed in the back. "So what's the verdict on the Junkers?" he asked Dicky.

"Bit of a challenge I'm afraid." Dicky put the jeep in gear and headed toward two small hangars on the far side of the ramp. "The kite was in reasonable shape and I thought we were home free. But we did a short check flight and found the port engine is leaking oil badly."

"How bad?" Jack asked.

"Bad enough that only a fool would try to fly it for longer than ten minutes."

"Shit," Jack said, his mind already trying to figure out options.

"We've got one chance," Dicky continued. "On the Hudson is a part that our mechs thought would be a suitable replacement for the oil cooler that's leaking on the Junkers. If we can jury rig it on the engine we might be in business."

"A British part on a German engine," Karl asked.

70

"Engines are engines," Dicky replied. The oil pressure and quantity on both engines are similar. If the fittings are compatible it should work."

"How long before you know," Jack asked.

The jeep stopped in front of the partially open hangar doors.

"They're starting right now. We should be ready to spin the engine in two or three hours. If it runs good on a ground check I'll take it for a test hop. We could be ready to depart in four to five hours."

Jack looked at his watch. That gave them about an hour of leeway if the repair worked. If not he had to come up with a back up plan.

"We could jump from the Hudson. Not desirable but we'd still be on the ground."

Karl got out of the back seat. "Have to be a night jump."

Jack turned to Dmitri. "Are you ready for a night jump?"

The Russian nodded. "I've made several in the past few years."

"Dicky, can you get your lads to line up three parachutes for us and we'll need one equipment bag with a chute."

The four men walked into the hangar to see a dark green twin engine aircraft sitting with two wooden platforms under the port engine. The Luftwaffe markings seemed strange and hostile as they walked by several mechanics working on the engine. Nearby two other men unpacked a wooden crate.

"You can set up in that far office, Jack." Dicky pointed at a set of double doors that opened into the hangar. "I'll get Sergeant McKenzie working on the jump gear."

"Dicky, we'll need the equipment bags in there. Let us know about the engine as soon as you can."

"Right."

As Jack opened the door a very distinct tobacco aroma greeted him.

Group Captain Toms sat in a high backed leather chair smoking a white stemmed pipe and reading from a notebook.

"Hello, gentlemen," Toms said standing up as the Karl and Dmitri entered the room.

"Group Captain, I didn't expect to find you here," Jack said, not thinking how it sounded.

"Standish was scheduled to go with Dicky but he managed to hurt himself in a bicycle accident of all things. I'm the only other Hudson qualified pilot who speaks German. Besides I flew in and out of Germany a great deal before the war. And if it's anything like last time I wouldn't want to miss the show."

Toms and Dicky Thompson had flown a Hudson into Germany to rescue Karl and Jack on their first mission together. The actual extraction included a battle between their escorting Mustang fighters and several trucks of German soldiers. As Toms was to say latter, "It was like something out of the bloody cinema."

"Dicky told us about the problem on the Junkers. If we can't use the German aircraft, we'll have to jump from the Hudson," Jack told Toms.

"Is the time that critical? If we delayed twenty four hours I'm certain we can get the Junkers ready to go."

The door opened and a young man stuck his head in. "Sir, we have the equipment bags."

"Put them on that long table," Karl said.

After the two men left, Jack said, "The Russians are pressing hard from the east. We think getting in and back out as quickly as possible is crucial. I'd rather have your men making sure the Junkers is ready to pull us out of there when the time comes. There are risks to jumping but we've all done it."

Karl and Dmitri unpacked the first bag. He removed camouflaged SS combat uniforms which had been accurately reproduced at a special MI-6 workshop in Surrey.

"We brought along Luftwaffe flight suits if you want them," Jack told Toms. "Our intent is to exit with engines running and have you airborne as soon as possible. But if something happens and you have to shut down, the flight suits might be useful. Of course if you're caught in a German flight suit it will go very bad."

"I'll think it over."

On the table three SS uniforms lay next to Walther P-38 pistols and MP-40 machine pistols. German parachute helmets with camouflage covers were stacked next to black jump boots.

"Looks like you chaps are serious," Dicky joked as he entered to see their gear on the table.

"Just a walk through the country," Karl said.

"Here are the latest charts and photos of the Seelow landing area. You might want to select a jump zone."

Wing Commander Toms and Squadron Leader Thompson joined Jack at a small desk. Karl and Dmitri stood looking over Jack' shoulder.

Chapter Nine

Posen
East Prussia
April 1945

Colonel Sergei Volkonsky climbed down the short ladder from the rear hatch of the olive drab Dakota transport. Low clouds scudded across the sky. Volkonsky was tired and the gray weather depressed him. Why was he here? A priority message had only told him to be at the Leipzig airport.

Looking across the ramp he noticed a small black sedan, which looked like a pre-war Polski FIAT, parked near the port wingtip. Standing behind the car he saw Nikolay Kalinin. The expensive overcoat could not disguise the man's corpulent figure. Volkonsky always thought of Kalinin as a human who looked more like a pig than a man with his upturned nose and jowly face. At least he now knew who was behind his orders to fly from Leipzig to Posen. Kalinin was the "black messenger" of Lavrenty Beria.

Trying to maintain a mask of indifference Volkonsky walked over to the car. He'd known Kalinin for many years although neither would ever call each other a friend.

"Kalinin, I would not have expected to find you so far from Moscow."

"Comrade Colonel, please get into the car."

So that's how it's to be, Volkonsky thought. Everyone who worked for Beria knew this day might come. He'd lasted longer than most.

The car left the ramp, turning onto a perimeter road and accelerating toward a group of buildings on the far side of the airport. The silence in the car didn't seem unusual to Volkonsky. This was how it always played out, each man knowing what would happen. In the past Volkonsky had performed these same duties for Beria.

Accepting his fate, Colonel Sergei Volkonsky stared straight ahead. He wouldn't give Kalinin the courtesy of conversation. There was nowhere to run, nothing he could do to escape the long reach of the NKVD. This is Ivanov's fault he thought, if only Dmitri had been successful on the Falkenberg.

Their destination was a two story brick building with only minor damage. A single soldier with a rifle slung over his shoulder guarded the main entrance. No worries in the world Volkonsky observed to himself, seeing the young man standing at rigid attention. All he has to do is to follow the orders of his sergeant and try to survive the war. Apparently that is something I won't do he thought ironically. The colonel dies and the private lives.

Kalinin exited the car and Volkonsky followed, using all the discipline he could muster. Normally a single shot to the back of the head. It will be over quickly, he told himself, but his heart still pounded. The door closed behind him and his eyes adjusted to the dim corridor.

75

He followed the short emissary from Moscow. I will die with dignity he told himself, show that pig Kalinin how a soldier accepts death.

"If you please," Kalinin said, indicating he should enter a single door off the corridor.

To Sergei Volkonsky's surprise, there was no one waiting in the room, only a desk with two chairs.

"Have a seat, Colonel." The fat man removed his overcoat and hung it on a wall hook.

Kalinin produced a manila envelope which had two diagonal red stripes across each side indicating a top secret document within. Withdrawing a sheet of paper the fat man began to read, "Moscow has been informed by a highly reliable source that Major Dmitri Ivanov is now at a country estate in England. This location is the headquarters of an operative group belonging to MI-6. The source goes on to say that the Major is there voluntarily and has been offered the opportunity to work for this group."

Volkonsky heard the words but found them hard to comprehend.

"Needless to say Marshall Beria is rather unhappy about this turn of events," Kalinin continued, the paper now lying on the desk.

Volkonsky's mind raced. MI-6? Dmitri is with the British Secret Service? The report seemed beyond ludicrous. It made no sense at all. He'd known Dmitri for years. He couldn't have been an agent for the British. Or could he?

"Do you have any comment?"

"What would you have me say?"

"Colonel, one of your main assistants is found working for British Intelligence and you don't find that unusual? Perhaps you'd like to tell the Marshall it means nothing. An important mission not only fails, but the man you handpicked to lead the mission now works for the other side!" Kalinin's voice had risen to a climax as his hand slammed down on the table.

Volkonsky's anger flared. "Dmitri Ivanov has been a loyal and successful member of this organization for over ten years. He's been decorated as a Hero of the Soviet Union and risked his life in missions against the Germans numerous times. Why do you now think he has switched allegiance? Perhaps he was forced into a situation that he could only deal with by pretending to join them." That must be it, Volkonsky thought. He knew Dmitri Ivanov, and he knew in his heart that he had not been working for the British or anyone else.

"An entertaining tale. But the Marshall tends to believe the worst about people until proved clearly wrong. Major Ivanov may very well be playing some game, but it is without the authority of Moscow and that has signed his death warrant."

Small buds were beginning to show on the tree branches highlighted by Moscow's setting sun. Across the city, people were ready for the end of the harsh winter weather. Despite the drab life imposed by the demands of war, the citizens of the capital seemed to be hopeful. Spring was upon them and the armies of the Soviet Union were almost to Berlin.

Lavrenty Beria should have been pleased. Franklin Roosevelt was out of the picture and two Soviet Army groups were poised on the Oder, ready for the final thrust into Germany. But sitting in the back of his black Ford touring car, the man responsible for the security of the state was in a foul mood. His meeting with Stalin had gone much as he expected it would. The dictator was in no mood to be told that the German atomic scientists from the Falkenberg facility had been captured by the British. What Beria had not told Stalin was that Major Dmitri

Ivanov was now apparently working for British Intelligence. I will see that man dead, he told himself. The car turned down Lubyanskiy Proyezd toward Lubyanka but Beria didn't notice.

His assistant was waiting as the car pulled into the interior drive. Vasily opened the door to the Ford.

"Get me Rostov," he barked at the young man and walked past him, entering the doors held open by two uniformed security guards.

Konstantin Rostov entered Beria's large third floor office to find the Marshall standing with arms folded looking out his window.

"Sir, we just received a message from Oscar."

Beria turned, his expression showing the fury that he was trying to contain.

"Read it."

Opening the binder Rostov began to read, "Information from an informant within MI-6 indicates that Ivanov has left England for Germany. Subject is in company with two senior MI-6 operatives. Informant believes the intent is for all three to infiltrate behind the lines, target: Berlin. Actual mission is unknown. Will attempt to obtain additional information. More to follow as soon as possible."

Beria walked over to Rostov and took the paper, reading it again silently. "What are they up to?" He asked, more to himself than Rostov and walked back to his desk. "Why would British Intelligence try to put two agents and Ivanov into Berlin now?"

"Secret negotiations?" Rostov offered.

"No, there are easier ways to make contact." Beria sat down, staring ahead as he went over the possibilities in his mind.

"Perhaps assassination?" Rostov asked.

"Possibly. But why take Ivanov?"

"I don't know, sir."

"Do the British want to eliminate someone they don't want us to capture?" Now Beria could see some possible reasons. "Or destroy some evidence we might find? Perhaps they need Ivanov as a translator or he has some special knowledge."

"Yes, sir," Rostov agreed, "That is possible."

"Our major offensive across the Oder begins tomorrow morning. I want Volkonsky across the river as soon as we can get Malenkov there. If the British and Ivanov are headed for Berlin, they're in for a surprise. I want full descriptions of these agents and Ivanov distributed to all military police and state security detachments. I will catch our errant Major. Tell Volkonsky not to fail me this time."

Rostov understood Beria's meaning.

Sergei Volkonsky wasn't asleep when he heard a knock on the door. Although the light was out in the small room, sleep had evaded him for the last two hours. He kept going over in his mind what Kalinin had told him. The "defection" simply didn't make sense unless Dmitri was trying to dupe the British. What possible reason would he have to join the side everyone knew would be their next enemy. He couldn't have been a deep plant agent, Volkonsky had personally vetted Ivanov. Could I have been that wrong about a man I've known for years, he asked himself?

The door swung open allowing a pale light to filter in from the hallway.

"Comrade Colonel, you're wanted downstairs," a young NKVD Sergeant said quietly.

"Kalinin?"

"Yes, sir."

"Tell him I'll be there in ten minutes."

He found Nikolay Kalinin sitting at the same desk as before, the ashtray now full of cigarette butts. The fat man looked like he hadn't gone to bed. Kalinin handed him a piece of paper from the documents laying on the table.

"Read this, we just decoded it from Moscow."

As his eyes moved back and forth across the typed words Volkonsky realized what the message was telling him. Beria had proof that Ivanov was helping the British. And now it was his job to fix the problem. He could see Lavrenty Beria's face and it chilled him.

"We're arranging air transport from here to the forward observation strip near Kostryzn. There you'll be met by a commando unit that has been working behind the German lines for the last several months. Their job is to get you and Malenkov across the Oder and behind the German lines." Kalinin handed Volkonsky a thick envelope. "Here's your authorization. It will give you the highest priority for equipment and support." The fat man paused. "Marshall Beria is a very generous man, certainly more than I would have been." He smiled slightly. "You leave in thirty minutes. Rostov's agent has a plant within the British group that's running the operation. We'll pass on any information that might help you find the traitor."

Volkonsky turned and left the room without speaking. It had been a long time since he had seen Gregori Malenkov. There were few better agents in the NKVD. Perhaps with Gregori's help he would find Dmitri and survive Beria's wrath. Of course Malenkov could also be his executioner, only time would tell.

As the open scout car bounced around the perimeter road leading back to the airfield, Sergei Volkonsky made a vow to himself. If Dmitri Ivanov was in Germany he would find him, find out why he had done what he had done, then kill him. A black rage filled his soul. First

I'll kill Ivanov, then I'll kill Kalinin he told himself, the thought pleasing him.

"Major Haselman, I see from the security log that you left the bunker for thirty six hours earlier this week. Rather unusual absence for someone who is responsible for the Fuhrer's communications." Standartenfuhrer Ernst Mueller sat opposite Willy reading from a small notebook.

"I was summoned by my father. I did get General Molder's permission before I left." Willy knew his story would check out but he also hated to come to the attention of Mueller who was known for his suspicion of everyone. Some threads from the July plot must still exist and anyone could still be summarily executed without appeal.

"And you went alone?" The fat man smiled at Willy.

"I went with my father's orderly, Sergeant Dieter Hoffman."

Mueller wrote something in the notebook.

"That's all for now. I may have additional questions for you later."

Willy watched the door close. Mueller could be a problem, he thought. He looked at his watch knowing that he needed to leave in two hours. Perhaps he could get out of the bunker without signing the log. In any case he must be at the house on the lake outside Strausberg by sunrise. That would depend on getting out of the bunker and finding the vehicle his father was sending. Willy continued to ponder the biggest issue, could he violate his oath of loyalty?

Dicky Thompson swung the door of the office open to find Jack, Karl and Dmitri already dressed in their German camouflage uniforms.

"My God," he said, staring at the three men.

"Takes a bit of getting used to," Terry Toms said from behind the large desk.

Dicky saw that the Wing Commander was wearing the dark blue Luftwaffe flying coveralls. His look prompted Toms to get up.

"Well, what do you think? Do I look like a convincing Luftwaffe transport pilot?"

"As long as you don't talk to anyone, Skipper."

Toms replied in harsh German, "You will stand at attention when addressing your superior."

All of the men looked at Toms in surprise.

"I do know the language, gentlemen. Just haven't had much of a need to use it in the last five years."

Jack laughed and the others smiled as Toms turned to Dicky.

"What's you verdict on the Junkers?" he asked.

"Give the lads an hour to fuel and service her," Dicky replied. "No problem at all with the oil pressure during the flight. Checked for any leaks on the post flight and everything looks clean."

"So our parachute plan won't be needed?" Jack asked.

Dicky shook his head. "I just hope they've picked a decent landing strip."

"We'll know in about six hours," Karl said, looking at his watch.

Jack walked over to the wall map. Using his thumb and little finger as a crude divider, he measured the distance on the map.

"Two hundred and fifty miles or so?" he asked Dicky.

"Actually it's a little more from the airport to the landing site. Weather expects mostly crosswinds so I'm estimating an hour and a half, takeoff to landing. That assumes we don't run into any problems airborne and there's no weather on top of Seelow." Dicky said, his tone now serious.

"What are they calling?" Jack asked, knowing that Dicky would understand the question.

"Scattered to broken clouds. Nothing specific on the ceiling but they don't think we'll see anything lower than a few thousand feet. A front went through this afternoon so we got a break." The message from the network had said there would be smoke pots to outline the landing area with headlights pointing in the landing direction. With a little illumination from the moon, the landing now seemed feasible.

"So we need to be wheels up by 0130 to make our 0300 land time."

"Right."

Jack followed Karl over to the short couch that stood against the wall under the largest window. His friend stretched back on one end and Jack dropped into the other. He looked at Karl, who now had his eyes closed. Jack thought back on their previous missions and how their friendship and respect had deepened. How can you come to embrace a man who had been your sworn enemy he had continued to asked himself? The answer was always the same – because it's Karl Dietrich.

"You're thinking too much again, my friend."

Jack looked over and Karl grinned at him.

"Occupational hazard I suspect."

Karl was silent for a moment. Although there were other men in the room, this conversation was only between the two of them. "This one scares me more than anything else I've ever done," he said quietly.

Knowing what they had done together and what Karl had done on his own, the words shocked Jack.

"We've talked about all the risks. What still bothers you?" Jack asked.

"It's a completely unknown situation. Crete, Norway, Russia, even with you there was a good idea of what was happening, who were the players." Karl sat up slightly but kept his voice low. "Germany's collapsing. The country and system I knew is coming apart. Fear and chaos breed irrationality and danger. That's what bothers me. We don't know what we'll find on the other end."

Jack said nothing. Karl was right. But both of them knew it wouldn't keep them from getting on that aircraft and flying into the unknown. Perhaps it was better to not think about things too much.

"What the hell," Karl said, "We'll figure it out." He closed his eyes.

Willy Haselman climbed the steep steps to the upper level security checkpoint, his boots rasping on the cold concrete. Trying to stay relaxed, he knew the next few minutes were critical. All visitors in and out of the bunker were checked by the SS guards and logged into the desk record. He didn't need any questions from Mueller about his whereabouts. The duty roster listed Sergeant Talbe as the senior guard on duty. Over the last two years Willy had become friends with the Sergeant who had also been wounded in Russia. Both men were from Bavaria, their hometowns only seven miles apart. He had never tried to use that friendship but now he had no choice.

At the top of the stairs, he swung the steel door open to see Heinz Talbe sitting at the guard desk.

"Good evening, Herr Major." Talbe smiled as he stood up.

Willy returned the smile and walked to the desk before he spoke in a quiet voice. "I need to duck out for a while but I'm trying to be very quiet about it."

Talbe looked slightly surprised. "I'm not sure what you mean."

"I'm going to visit a woman and I'm not sure the brass would be happy about that."

Sitting down, Talbe said quietly, "In these difficult times it is possible for procedures to break down. I see no need to record your departure," his tone now conspiratorial. "When will you return?

"1000."

"Very well. I'll come back up to relieve Hunsaker at 0730 and be on duty until 1200."

"My girl appreciates your discretion, Heinz."

"Good evening, Herr Major."

Turning up the collar on his overcoat Willy pushed into the courtyard and moved toward Heiserstrasse. Still unsure what he would do, the young Major walked into the darkness.

Chapter Ten

40 Miles East of Dortmund
April 1945

The interior of the Junkers had surprised Jack. The cleanliness told him it must have been a VIP transport. He doubted if these seats had ever seen combat troops or wounded men. The three men sat in different rows, each at a small round window. The darkened cabin was silent except for the sound of the engines.

The takeoff had been uneventful. During the power up and climb out only a smooth roar came from the two radials. Now level at 4,000 feet the small aircraft cut through the scattered clouds heading east. Dicky's navigation track would take them north of Berlin then south paralleling the Oder to Seelow.

Jack remembered another flight like this, his first mission with Karl. They had been aboard a Lancaster bomber which blended into a bomber raid on Leipzig. They had been dropped into the countryside outside of Posen to rendezvous with a partisan group. Once on the ground it had become clear that Jack had gained a true comrade. The mission had been a success, disrupting the German's plans to arm their V-2 rocket with a chemical warhead. Karl had gone behind the lines again, this time with Pamela Thompson. They had impersonated a German scientist and his wife. The two had been landed on the Dutch coast, traveling by train to Leipzig then on to the Falkenberg compound. The entire compliment of scientists along with their records had been rescued and flown back to England.

Jack knew the success of those missions had made a huge difference in the lives of many people. This time he wasn't sure. What difference would it make if one man survived or not? He had to trust his Prime Minister. This mission was more political than military but he guessed that is what the future would hold. His organization would probably change as the war wound down and become a tool for political ends. But as they say, that was beyond his pay grade. Jack closed his eyes, the rhythm of the engines now part of the night.

Karl Dietrich looked down at the dark countryside and wondered what the future held for Germany. Always a realist, he knew that the victors would extract a terrible price from the vanquished. When the final tally was complete, how many German men and women would have died on the battlefield or in the flaming wreckage of Germany's cities? The hope of a generation wiped out, a country with a culture of enlightenment for hundreds of years descending into a world of brutal survival. Two million Russians now sat on the eastern shore of the Oder River ready to drive the final stake in Germany's heart. Remembering the devastation the Wermacht had visited on Russia he knew the retribution would be cruel and thorough. He'd done his best to end this war by helping the British. When he thought of what Sarin gas might have done to London he knew his decision to defect had been the right one. Now with the Falkenberg scientists safely in England he hoped the new terrible weapon would not end up under the control of Stalin. One final time into the battle, he thought. It seemed as if the war had gone on forever. Perhaps when this was over he would marry Eva. He smiled in the darkness. There was always something to kindle hope.

Martin Bormann, Dmitri thought as he sat back in the padded seat. It seemed inconceivable that he was in the company of an American in the Royal Navy, a former SS Colonel and on his way to rescue a man who had helped start the greatest war in history. He wondered what Sergei would think if he knew. His friend must consider him dead and just as well. Maybe someday they would meet again. Of all the men he had known, Sergei Volkonsky was his closest friend. That friendship had helped him succeed on many missions simply because he didn't want to let his friend down. But had he now betrayed that friendship? Surely Sergei would understand why he had acted as he did. What choice did he have? He knew the rest of the NKVD would condemn him instantly, but not his friend. Some things were stronger than ideology. He leaned back and closed his eyes, the questions still in his mind.

Waking from a light doze, Jack looked at the luminous dial on his German issue combat watch. They should be nearing Seelow soon. He pulled himself up and walked forward to the cockpit. Wing Commander Toms sat in the left seat, right hand on the yoke. Dicky held a small light on a folded chart. He looked back at Jack and grinned.

"You're in luck, my boy. Positive checkpoint on the west bank of the river. Right turn to 225 magnetic, Boss. As we roll out, Seelow will be on the nose at seventeen miles."

Bending down and looking out the cockpit windows Jack saw the clouds had thinned to a few scattered layers.

"I'll let them know."

As Jack turned to head back into the cabin he heard Toms reduce the power slightly and felt the attitude change.

"We're approaching Seelow. Weather looks all right," Jack said to Karl who simply nodded. He turned and stepped across the aisle to Dmitri. "It's time." Jack slid into his seat and found the seat belt. As he closed the latch he realized he was no longer nervous.

The moon's reflection off the largest lake west of the landing area caught Terry Tom's attention first.

"Two o'clock, looks like one of the lakes."

Dicky looked out and then back down at his chart. "Spot on."

The Junkers banked right and Toms reduced power to start a wide slow turn over the lake. Both men were looking back to the east for the landing area. Scattered clouds created a patchwork over the valley and neither man could see anything resembling the described site.

"It should be right there," Toms said, pointing just left of the Junker's nose.

"I agree. Don't see a bloody thing."

They flew straight ahead for thirty seconds before Toms began a turn to the left. "I'll come around again."

Dieter Hoffman lit the rolled up paper and tossed it into the metal bucket. The coal oil began to burn and the yellow flames climbed above the top of the bucket. Quickly he ran to the small Kubelwagen and drove south toward the far end of the large field. Overhead he could hear the sound of aircraft engines. The partially covered headlights cast strange patterns as he bounced across the rough ground toward the remaining oil filled buckets.

Dicky made his way aft in the aisle.

"Nothing down there, Jack. We're over the valley. Cross checked several navpoints but there's nothing on the ground."

"How's the fuel?"

"We've got another thirty or forty minutes before it gets tight," Dicky said.

Jack knew they could jump into the valley if necessary. Their parachutes lay in the last two rows of seats. But once on the ground they would have to find transportation and make their way to the rendezvous having never been there.

Karl had unstrapped and now leaned over the seat in front of Jack.

"What do you think?" he asked Karl.

"We can jump but we have to keep it tight. I don't want us spread all over the countryside."

Now Dmitri joined the group.

"We may be looking at a jump," Jack said to him.

"All right," he said as if it made no difference one way or the other.

"Dicky," Toms yelled from the front.

As Jack and Dicky returned forward they saw Terry pointing to three spots of light on the ground.

"Better late than never," Dicky said and slid into the co-pilot's seat.

Dieter Hoffman stood by the open door of the Kubelwagen, its headlights pointed across the field illuminating the first several hundred feet of low grass. He could hear the sound of the aircraft's engines. The noise increased and suddenly overhead a shape materialized in the moonlight. Clearing the vehicle by less than thirty feet the aircraft touched down at the extreme edge of the patch of light and rolled out on its landing.

In less than two minutes he saw the transport heading directly toward the lighted area. Both engines were turning at idle. Hoffman could see the grass being bent down by the prop wash as the aircraft pulled to within 100 feet before swinging sharply around aligning for takeoff.

The aft cabin hatch opened and a man jumped down. A second man followed and then a canvas bag. A third man was now on the ground, all three walking toward the lights. Each man carried a weapon slung over his shoulder and aimed directly at Dieter.

The engines ran up to full power as the men approached Hoffman. Behind them the Junkers rolled into the darkness, its engines echoing in the valley.

Hoffman wasn't sure what he had expected, but it wasn't what he saw. Moving toward him were three senior officers in Waffen SS combat uniforms. When the first man spoke the effect was complete.

"Have you seen any other troops in the area?" the tallest man asked.

The man's German was flawless and the tone of his voice made Hoffman respond automatically. "No, sir."

Karl helped Dmitri lift the equipment bag into the backseat of the small vehicle. Jack said to Hoffman, "Let's get out of here."

Chapter Eleven

The Oder River
April 1945

"Captain Kulyagin, your job is to get us to the other side of the Oder and past enemy lines. Once you've completed that, I want part of the team to establish a safe area on the western shore for our return." Sergei Volkonsky stood next to the hood of a small truck shining a flashlight on an unfolded map. A tall man stood next to the Colonel. His combat parka carried the insignia of a Soviet Spetnaz commando unit.

"When do you want to move out, sir?"

"As soon as Colonel Malenkov arrives. I'll let you know."

"Any idea when that might be, Colonel?"

Volkonsky thought of the flamboyant Ukrainian agent. "I suspect we won't wait long."

Lieutenant Fedov walked up to the two and saluted.

"Sir, we just received a radio message that Colonel Malenkov should be here within the half hour."

"Thank you, Lieutenant. Why don't you and Sergeant Ruess go get something hot to drink while we wait?"

An artillery piece fired to the south of them and in quick succession the single shot became a rolling barrage as over 1400 heavy guns began covering fire for the first assault wave across the Oder. Volkonsky was not a stranger to a battlefield but the scale of the bombardment was hard to comprehend. The firing blended into a deafening roar accompanied by the arcing flights of Katusha rockets.

Two Soviet Army groups were beginning the last push toward the hated capital of their blood enemy. Many of these men had defended Moscow, Leningrad or Stalingrad and fought their way back across their own country to exact a terrible toll on the German aggressors. Now it was time to finish that long fight.

Gregori Malenkov took one last drag on his Lucky Strike and exhaled slowly. The Americans make great trucks and cigarettes, he thought, but give me a Russian tank anytime. He threw the cigarette on the ground and walked into the large tent. A large sign identified the tent as the sector command post.

"I'm looking for Colonel Volkonsky," he said to the young officer sitting at a small wooden desk.

The young man stood up and saluted. "Colonel Volkonsky is in the next tent, sir."

Malenkov looked around. One young sub-lieutenant and three enlisted men, none of them older than eighteen he guessed. Turning without answering he wondered where the adults were tonight?

Pushing the tent flap open Malenkov stepped inside and saw Sergei Volkonsky pouring coffee into a metal cup.

"Lieutenant, would you and Sergeant Ruess please leave us for a few minutes?"

Malenkov watched the two men leave but said nothing.

Volkonsky took a drink. "There's coffee," he said, watching Malenkov unbutton his overcoat.

"Any good?" the Malenkov asked.

"It's hot."

Malenkov poured a cup and sat down on a wooden crate opposite Volkonsky.

"They only gave me the basic requirements. Sounded interesting, but not something I would have expected."

"Nor would I, Gregori Alexivich. It seems I've been given a chance to redeem myself. And you have a chance to risk your life to save mine. The irony is spectacular."

"My orders came from the top," Malenkov said.

Volkonsky nodded. "Beria."

"Does it mean what I think?"

"I think so," Sergei said.

"She would enjoy this I think."

Volkonsky remembered her sense of humor. Yes, she would enjoy this. He had taken Katrina away from Malenkov. Now his life depended on the man he had jilted. The irony was sharp.

Both men sat silently for a moment, each remembering Katrina but in a different way.

"So what would our leader have us do?" Malenkov said, lighting a cigarette.

94

"Find Dmitri Ivanov and the British Intelligence team he's working with."

The shock on Malenkov's face registered in his eyes but he said nothing.

Volkonsky drained his coffee and reached behind him for a canteen. "Before I tell you, I need a drink." He uncapped the canteen and poured a strong measure of vodka into the cup.

Gregori finished his coffee and held out his cup which Sergei filled.

"Ivanov was sent on a mission behind German lines to capture a group of German scientists. They were intercepted by the British and apparently he decided to switch sides. We have intelligence that tells us he and a small team are being inserted near Berlin. We're not sure why, but it must be important. It will give us a chance to grab Ivanov."

"Do you think he turned? I've known Dmitri almost as long as you. He'd never go over."

Volkonsky took a drink. "I felt the same way. But the evidence says otherwise. All we can do is find him and bring him back."

Malenkov laughed. "We'd have better luck finding a single wheat stalk on the steppes. There are a half a million German soldiers being pushed back on Berlin by two million Russians. How in the hell do we find one man?"

"There's an intelligence source in England we hope will provide some direction."

"My God."

"And we need to move out as quickly as possible. Did you bring your equipment?"

"There are uniforms and equipment for seven. Is that enough?"

Volkonsky nodded. "I'll talk to our young commando. By the way, I have a real German Sergeant working for us. He was with Dmitri on the mission."

"Then let's get busy."

Chapter Twelve

Lake Straussee
Brandenburg, Germany
April 1945

The Kubelwagen turned down a dark and narrow driveway lined with trees. Even with the shaded headlights, Dieter Hoffman knew his way to the cottage. The small one story bungalow had belonged to the Haselman family for two generations. In better times the General would spend summer afternoons fishing from the small dock, enjoying the beautiful deep blue lake.

Traffic, once they turned on the main east west road, had been light, mostly military supply trucks and the occasional automobile. They had made good time and now Hoffman slowed the Kubelwagen and turned left into a graveled parking area next to the cottage.

"This is where we will wait," he said as the engine stopped.

"Karl, look around," Jack directed as he got out, his machine pistol at the ready. "I'll check the house."

"Right."

Hoffman led the other two to the front door which he unlocked and entered.

Ten minutes later the men sat in the small main room of the cottage. Several candles provided enough light for Karl to operate the small radio transmitter.

"Message sent and acknowledged," he said, switching the main power switch off.

"Now we wait," Jack said. "Sergeant, I have coffee if you can get some hot water."

"Yes, sir," Hoffman answered automatically, knowing this man was a British operative, but unable to ignore the German uniform.

The four of them had just sat down with china mugs of steaming coffee when Hoffman said, "I hear something."

They all stood and moved to the windows, Karl and Dmitri carrying their weapons.

Jack followed the Sergeant who opened the door several inches. Parked next to their Kubelwagen a small Porsche sedan switched off its engine. They watched a single man walk toward the cottage. The Sergeant assured them it was the man they were expecting.

Willy Haselman stepped into the cottage, his eyes quickly taking in the men with Hoffman. Not sure what he had expected, he now felt very unsure of himself. These men were Germany's enemies and he was here to help them.

Moving into the living room he now could see the other two men wore German combat uniforms and were holding machine pistols.

"My name is Stewart," Jack said in fluent German.

"You are American?"

"Commander, Royal Navy." Jack answered.

Willy hesitated then said, "Haselman, Major Wilhelm Haselman."

"Are you related to General Haselman?" Karl asked from behind him.

Willy turned in surprise, answering quietly, "He is my father."

"I know the General. He's a good soldier and a good German."

"And you are?" Willy asked.

"Dietrich, Karl Dietrich."

Willy looked at the man's hard face in the candlelight. It was Karl Dietrich, a man he knew by reputation. He looked at the other man who remained standing by himself at the window.

"Our colleague is Dmitri Ivanov, formerly Major Ivanov of the Soviet secret police," Karl said.

Willy turned back to Jack. "I have been instructed to provide you with whatever help you need." The tone told all of them that this man was not totally convinced he was doing the right thing.

"How much have you been told?" Jack asked.

"That you are trying to get Bormann out of Berlin."

Jack paused, "Please sit down, Major."

As Haselman turned in the candlelight, they could see his right arm was frozen by his side, the fingers drawn up into a tight fist.

"This is very important for many reasons which I can't divulge," Jack continued. "But I hope that you realize your father wouldn't have agreed to this without believing the same thing."

"He told me it was important for Germany and I am still a German officer." The combative tone remained in his voice. "What do you need?"

"We need to find a way to get a message to Bormann. Do you know if he is still in Berlin?"

Willy nodded, "I saw him yesterday."

Karl broke in, "You were in the bunker?"

Willy turned a wry smile, evident even in the candle light. "I am the Communications Officer for the Fuhrerbunker."

Ivanov laughed. "Luck of the British."

"You have access to the bunker?" Jack asked.

"That's where I live and work."

Jack leaned back against the chair. "How long before you need to be back?"

"One hour before I need to leave."

"Gentlemen, let's come up with a plan now that we know what we're dealing with."

Phil Hatcher stood in front of the expanded chart of Berlin and pushed a colored pin into the map. He stepped back as Hiram Baker walked in with Admiral Walter Kaltenbach.

"Here's the position from their first transmission," he said.

Kaltenbach walked over, seeing the red pin on the edge of Lake Strausee just west of Strausberg.

"I've been there. There are some parts of the shore that are very sparsely populated. They must be at one of the lake cabins."

"Did they mention any problems?" Hiram asked.

Phil shook his head. "Nothing so far."

"We need to keep them advised on the big picture. I'm sure they're aware of the Russian offensive by now but let's send them everything we can find out."

"I'll have the support team put together a quick message. We'll have it on the air at the next transmission window," Hatcher said.

"Besides, I think our support team would like this update." He pulled the pin from the map.

The two other men smiled.

Hatcher walked down the hallway to a room set aside for mission support. Their job was to monitor all activity and coordinate any assistance necessary to complete the mission. Besides several communicators, two agents had been detailed to run the effort. This morning Eva Papenhausen was on watch, Pam Thompson would relieve her at 0800.

"Good morning, Fraulein."

Eva looked up and smiled. "Phil, please tell me you have some information."

"So far so good. They're on the ground and safely at the rendezvous point. No word on their contact person but my understanding was they weren't really sure how long it would take to meet up with him."

"Anything we can do to update the map?" she asked. Behind her stood an easel holding a large map of Berlin and the surrounding territory.

"Here's the message. I didn't decode the coordinates. I'll let you do that and post it."

Eva nodded, taking the single piece of paper.

"They're doing fine, stop worrying," Hatcher told her, having seen the look in her eyes.

"I suppose I should be used to this, but I don't think I ever will."

"I know," he said.

Using the mission specific MI-6 code, Eva translated the random numbers into a set of coordinates. In a moment, she had placed a red push pin in the map on the southern end of a large lake outside the

101

town of Strausberg in Brandenburg. Sitting down at the desk she looked at the map and wished she were dead.

Major General Haselman sat quietly as the Group Operations Officer briefed Generaloberst Gotthard Heinrici, overall commander of German forces facing the Soviet onslaught. Both men looked tired, the strain of recent months taking a terrible toll.

"Following the preparatory artillery bombardment, units of the 5th Shock Army and 8th Guards Army crossed the Oder River, enveloping the area north and south of the autobahn. They have broken through our outer defenses and are moving east toward the Heights. We estimate over 150,000 men will be on this side of the river by late morning. Our main defensive positions escaped initial artillery damage but we expect them to come under both tank and unit artillery fire within the hour."

The Group Operations Officer returned to his seat and sat down uneasily.

Heinrici turned to his Chief of Staff. "Well, General, it appears it has finally begun."

Haselman nodded. "The Russians may win. But it will cost them heavily to break our line."

Both men knew that there was nothing that could be done to save Berlin or Germany. The strength of the Red Army was too overwhelming for the German forces remaining after the last year of the war. But they would do their best to delay the enemy. That would allow more Germans to flee to the west and the American Army.

The General thought it strange. He hated the Russians but hardly knew the Americans. The only time he'd ever met an American had been during the 1930's in Berlin. They seemed nice enough at the time, perhaps too nice. Maybe they were going to be no different than the Russians in victory. The end of a war as brutal as this one would bring out the worst in victorious soldiers. The last war ended badly and this war was the result. Was modern man doomed to fight war after war until all mankind was exterminated? Albert Haselman felt tired to the very center of his soul.

"General, I'm going to move to the forward command post just north of Seelow. I'd like you north of the highway. Stay in contact by radio and let me know what you see as they move west."

"As you wish," Haselman said.

The two men stood, followed by the remainder of the staff.

Heinrici turned to the group of thirty senior officers and aides. "Gentlemen, this will be a time of trial for Germany. All we can do is maintain our discipline and fight as hard as German soldiers have always done. After that it is in God's hands. I wish you all well." He turned and offered his hand to Haselman, whom he had known for thirty years. "Good by, my friend."

"Until we meet again."

Heinrici smiled at his friend. "Until we meet again."

Chapter Thirteen

Albermarle Street
London
April 1945

Eva looked up and down the street as she climbed the steps of the two story brick row house. Following instructions from Phillip Kent, she had driven into the city after her shift in the operations center. Knocking three times on the wood door she waiting in the cool morning for a response.

Phillip Kent opened the door. "Good morning, my dear. Do come in."

The small living room contained a worn couch and two armchairs. The house smelled musty with an odor of tobacco in the background.

"I hope you didn't mind a meeting place a bit off the beaten track." Kent smiled as he sat down in an armchair.

"What do you want?"

"Sit down, Eva. And don't take that tone with me."

She sat down on the couch, placing her handbag on the floor next to her feet.

"I'm here because I have no choice."

"That's quite right. And unless you would like to end up at the end of a rope I suggest you do what you're told."

She looked at him with loathing in her eyes.

"Now that we have that out of the way tell me about the mission that Stewart is on."

"Why should you have any need to know what MI-6 is doing?"

"That is none of your concern. All you need to know is that MI-5 is tired of being trumped by MI-6. When the war is over one bureau will eventually emerge as the lead agency for intelligence. I intend that will be MI-5 and someday I will direct the entire intelligence effort of England. So you will tell me what I need to know and you'll stay off the gallows."

Eva knew he was right. She had made a terrible mistake years ago that she couldn't ever escape. Now she had to betray Jack Stewart's trust in her and Karl's love. But what choice did she have?

"What do you want to know?"

"Where is the team and what is their mission?"

She hesitated, everything in her telling her not to say a word but she knew she was trapped.

"The team is east of Berlin in German held territory."

"Where exactly?"

Eva wondered why he would want that type of detail but she knew it made no difference, she had gone too far already.

"In a small cottage on the shore of Lake Strausee, near Strausberg."

"What are they doing there?" Kent felt the power he held over this woman and how this information would be received in Moscow.

"They are trying to extract someone from Berlin."

"Who?"

"That I don't know. No one knows except the team and the Admiral."

Kent wondered if she was lying. "Show me exactly where they're located."

Eva felt like she was slipping down a terrible slope as she picked up a map and took the offered pencil from Kent.

Twenty minutes later she emerged from the row house. Glancing north on the street she turned and walked rapidly south.

Phil Hatcher waited until she disappeared around the corner before he started the small sedan and did a u-turn heading toward Baker Street.

Sergei Volkonsky knelt behind a large pine tree, a set of German binoculars focused on the small clearing below him. He could see eight German soldiers standing next to two vehicles. Neither engine was running and the men seemed to be discussing a large map which lay on the hood of a small scout car. A large general purpose truck was parked behind the first vehicle, a large tarp covering the contents of the truck bed.

"The Colonel and I will go down first," he told Captain Kulyagin. "Have your men follow in combat spread. When I'm ready, I'll take out as many as I can with the first burst. Tell your men to be ready to kill the rest. Remind them we need those vehicles, try not to damage them. Understood?"

Kulyagin nodded.

"You ready?" Sergei asked Malenkov.

Gregori Malenkov wore the uniform of a Major in the Wermacht. Each of the four commandos wore German infantry uniforms, giving the appearance that of a small reconnaissance team. Volkonsky, dressed as a Sergeant, carried an MP-40 sub-machine gun as did each of the four commandos.

Malenkov motioned one of the commandos forward. "You're on point. Stay away from the Germans, act like you're on watch."

"Yes, sir," the man said as he broke cover and moved down the gentle slope to the clearing.

Malenkov followed, heading directly for the cluster of men. Four paces behind him Volkonsky led the remaining commandos and Sergeant Ruess.

"Patrol coming in," Malenkov yelled at the men standing near the vehicles. Other than curious looks, none of them seemed alarmed.

One man detached himself from the group and walked toward Malenkov. The Russian could see the soldier was young but wore the insignia of an Oberleutnant. Other than a holstered pistol, the officer carried no weapons. He saluted when he saw Malenkov's rank.

"Sir, we're from the regimental supply depot. We have ammunition for three battalions but can't find them."

Malenkov returned the salute. "The only troops we've seen in the last two hours have been Russians, Lieutenant. I suggest you turn around and head west as fast as you can."

The look of alarm on the young man's face showed he understood the danger he was in this close to the fighting.

"Yes, sir, immediately."

"Lieutenant, these are all your men?" He gestured to the seven men standing next to the larger truck.

"Yes, sir, just drivers and guards."

"Then there's room for my men also."

A smile appeared on the man's face. "Of course, sir."

As the young German officer turned back toward his men Malenkov nodded to Volkonsky, who raised his weapon and began firing in one motion. The other commandos knelt and began firing at the compact group of drivers.

Volkonsky's burst hit the German officer in the back from only two meters distance. The impact of the bullets threw the Lieutenant forward, blood flying from multiple wounds in his back. Without pausing, Volkonsky turned slightly and continued firing into the drivers. The Germans were torn apart by the automatic weapon fire and were collapsing around each other.

Almost as if on signal, the firing stopped. The commandos quickly moved to form a secure perimeter as the two officers ran to the dead and wounded Germans.

Several of the men were moaning, all hit by multiple bullet wounds. Seeing no weapons evident Malenkov turned to Captain Kulyagin. "Have your men drag the bodies over to that ditch. Cover them up with tree branches and be ready to move in five minutes."

Volkonsky knelt down and spread a map on the ground. He put his finger in what he estimated was their current position.

"Gregori, take a look at this."

Malenkov leaned down to look at the map.

"We're approximately here. This is the estimated position of the British team. I make that 30 kilometers. With these vehicles we could be there in two to three hours."

"That depends on the Germans. I'd be surprised to have a clear road."

"I'd guarantee we won't. You better be convincing," Volkonsky said as he folded the map.

Behind them a single shot rang out from the ditch. Captain Kulyagin replaced his pistol in the holster and walked over to the two officers.

"We're ready to move out, sir."

Jack Stewart poured steaming coffee into a china mug as he looked out the small kitchen window. Behind him the rest of the team, including Dieter Hoffman slept fitfully, sprawled on the furniture in the living room. He thought back to the meeting with Major Haselman. The young man was a stroke of luck they hadn't expected. Direct access to Martin Bormann would streamline their effort to get him out of Berlin.

Their discussion had covered the SS security arrangements and normal routine within the bunker. There was still steady visitor traffic in and out of the bunker throughout the day. The Reichschancellery and several of the surrounding buildings were still being used by both the military and civil authorities. Although bomb damage throughout the city was extensive, the area immediately near the bunker remained relatively intact. At some point the area would come within range of long range Soviet artillery and rocket attack. When that happened the Major felt the access to and from the bunker would become very difficult. Contact with Bormann must take place quickly. Execution of their plan had to come in short order after that. Haselman had to make that connection and do it quickly.

"Any coffee left?" Karl Dietrich sounded sleepy and Jack wondered how he could go into a deep sleep anytime in any situation.

Filling a second cup, Jack handed it to his friend.

"Does it feel different being back in Germany?"

Karl took a deep drink.

109

"I thought about it last night as we drove past the military positions. This place is about to become a battle field. I wonder if the Germany of 1933 could have seen where the Nazis would take the country, would they have let them take power?"

"We have a saying that 'hindsight is 20/20.''

"I don't understand," Karl said.

"The past is always clear when seen from the future."

Karl laughed. "We have the same saying."

Dmitri Ivanov sat up in one of the chairs, rubbing his face vigorously. "Is it time?" he asked.

Jack handed him a cup of coffee.

"Let's be on the road by 1100."

Karl walked across the room and shook Dieter Hoffman's arm. "Sergeant, time to move out."

Hoffman opened his eyes slowly then as if he remembered where he was and with whom he sat up abruptly. "As you wish."

Thirty minutes later the four men had stowed their gear in the Kubelwagen and were heading down the gravel road toward the main highway.

"Slow down," Volkonsky said as he examined the map while glancing out at an upcoming intersection.

Captain Kulyagin eased up on the accelerator of the small car. Traffic had been heavy once they found the main autobahn, primarily military trucks moving to and from the front. Behind them the rumble of shelling told the story of the desperate struggle on the western bank of the Oder. An occasional tracked vehicle passed them heading for the front, the effort seeming futile after the lines of tanks they had seen ready to come across the river.

"Is that the road," Malenkov asked from the back seat.

"It looks like it. Captain, turn right up here."

Checking his watch, Volkonsky noted their trip had taken over three hours. He was thankful there had been little air activity while they had been on the autobahn. To a Red Air Force fighter bomber their vehicles would have been prime targets.

The vehicles turned out of the main traffic flow onto the intersecting road. A military policeman standing next to a large motorcycle watched the two vehicle pass then returned to watching the main road.

From the corner of his eye, Volkonsky watched the policeman looking for any sign of alarm. The Russian didn't look closely at the Kubelwagen which passed them going in the opposite direction but instead focused down the long road running along a line of tall trees. The cottage should be about two kilometers down this road on the end of an unimproved road, he thought the idea of finding Ivanov at the end of the road was strangely satisfying.

"My God," Dmitri said from behind Hoffman who turned the car west into the main traffic flow.

Both Jack and Karl turned to look at him.

For a moment he didn't speak, the reality of what he had just seen overwhelming him.

"Our mission just became much more complicated."

"What does that mean?" Jack asked.

In front of them a large truck ground its transmission, making Hoffman hit the brakes.

Ivanov seemed not to notice but continued, "He might have been wearing a German uniform, but I saw Colonel Sergei Volkonsky in the front seat of the vehicle we just passed. Behind the driver sat Colonel

Gregori Malenkov. I know both men well. They are NKVD and unless you believe in remarkable coincidences, they're after us."

"What?" Karl said, his voice harsh. "How could they know we're here? Only a very small group of people have any idea where we are right now. How would these men find that out?"

"I have no idea, Karl. But Volkonsky was my immediate superior and he's a trusted agent for Beria. Malenkov is the "fixer." He also works directly for Beria and those two would not be together unless something very important was up."

Jack sat in the front seat trying to take in what Ivanov was saying. Only the small ops group at Corry Woods knew where they were. The Admiral knew, as did Phil, Hiram and Erich. That was it. How could that info have made its way to the Russians?

"Why would the Russians send a team in ahead of their own offensive? They know they're going to take Berlin, why not wait until it's secured?"

"I think we have to assume they're after Dmitri," Jack said.

"There are much easier ways than running a covert operation in the middle of a major battle," Karl said.

Jack turned to look at his friend. "If they know where we are, they might know more about our mission."

The three men said nothing, each contemplating this change of events.

"I would agree, my Russian friend. This mission just became much more difficult."

After finding the cottage and securing the perimeter they had watched the cottage for thirty minutes for any sign of life. On signal Volkonsky and three other had entered the house carefully but found no one.

"We couldn't have missed them by much," Malenkov said, his hand on the half full pot of coffee. "It's still warm."

Volkonsky looked around for any evidence of a recent visit but saw nothing out of the ordinary. "They could be anywhere by now."

"I think we need to keep a watch on this place in case they come back. But we must contact control to see if they have any updates," Malenkov said.

"I agree. Captain, find a good observation point and we'll set up the radio. Once we've sent our message make sure the men get something to eat. It could be a long wait."

Chapter Fourteen

The Fuhrerbunker
16 April, 1945

Barely able to concentrate on what he was reading, Willy looked at the message log for the time he had been gone. Thankful that Sergeant Talbe had been at the security desk when he returned, he now waited to see if any other indication of his absence might surface. His mind kept returning to the meeting with the British. It was up to him to establish contact with Bormann. He then had to find some way to contact the team with updated information. What would the Minister say when he approached him? How do you tell the man who is closer to Adolph Hitler than anyone else in Germany that you are bringing a message from British Intelligence?

He was startled from his thoughts by the loud buzz of the phone.

"Major Haselman," he said.

"Major, this is Standartenfuhrer Mueller."

Willy detested the man. "What can I do for you?"

"I would like to review the communication log for the last 24 hours."

An unusual request, Willy thought, but not out of order for a security agent.

"Very well, I'll have it delivered to your office."

Mueller said quickly, "No need, I'll stop by your office in ten minutes."

Willy hung up the phone. Mueller wasn't a man to be trusted or let your guard down with.

"These are dangerous times," Mueller said as he read down the log book. "We can leave no stone unturned."

"No, sir," Willy said, wishing Mueller would come to the point.

"Tell me, Major, didn't you know von Quirnheim?

At the mention of one of the conspirators against Hitler, Willy felt uncomfortable. Did Mueller know something? Was he just playing with him or was he fishing?

"Why do you ask?"

Mueller looked up from the log book. "Why won't you tell me?"

Willy saw the malice in the man's eyes.

Herr Standartenfuhrer, I would be happy to tell you, it just seems such a strange question."

"Perhaps you have information you don't wish us to know."

"I knew Colonel von Quirnheim. We served together during the initial attack on Russia. He was wounded about the same time I was. We ended up in the military hospital in Katrinberg."

"So you were friends?"

Now anger replaced fear. "Yes, we were friends. But I didn't see him after the summer of 1943."

"Is that so?"

Willy said nothing and Mueller returned to reading the log book.

"And I understand your father knew General Olbricht very well."

Executed the same time as Klaus Von Stauffenberg, Olbricht was considered one of the main conspirators of the July plot. Olbricht and Albert Haselman had been close friends for over twenty years. Was this man trying to tie those threads together? Willy looked across the table at Mueller and knew that his life was in danger.

Phil Hatcher stood looking out the tall window in his office watching the panorama of a beautiful spring morning breaking across the Kent countryside. But the former Scotland Yard detective was oblivious to the scenery. His meeting the day before with Brigadier Greene bothered him more than he thought it should have. He knew his double role would now have to surface and that would affect his friendship with Jack Stewart, something he truly valued.

Three years ago when Stewart had just arrived from the States, Hatcher had been one of the individuals that Noel Greene offered to Jack as part of a new Section F. What Jack had never known was Phil's position in the counter-espionage section of MI-6. Phil had been tasked by Noel Greene to carefully watch the development of Section F as it grew and took on more sensitive operations. Greene did not want any problems with security to affect his new operation despite aggressive recruiting from outside MI-6.

In fact there had been one very serious incursion when a recruit turned out to be working for the Germans and feeding information to the Gestapo. They were able to feed her false information and subsequently terminate her. Phil had remained under cover while the Section F transitioned to the current Double 00 operation and Greene intended him to remain in place fulfilling the same function.

But he now had a problem that would not only destroy his cover but it also tear a member out of the team. Eva Papenhausen had become a key member of the entire operation and a close friend of most other team members. And the close personal relationship between Karl and Eva made things even more distasteful.

Greene had told him during their meeting that there had been some questions about Phillip Kent which they had been carefully examining. This development clearly indicated that Kent was working for the Soviets. And it appeared Eva was working for him. Why? He had to know.

He thought of Jack and Karl on the ground near Berlin, possibly compromised by Eva. Was Ivanov part of this or an unwitting victim? How did they find out the extent of Kent's involvement while still protecting Jack and Karl? Now operating under Noel Greene's direct orders, Phil's job was to coordinate efforts to shadow Kent as they tried to determine the extent of the damage.

"We just received a message they've moved into the city."

Phil snapped out of his thoughts as Hiram read from the message pad.

"Did they send a specific location?"

"Only that they are near the Brandenburg Gate."

"I'll take this down to the ops group," Baker said.

"No wait. I'll do it."

Baker looked mildly surprised but shrugged and handed the paper to Hatcher.

Thirty minutes later Hatcher handed Eva a message detailing the team's location in Berlin. It was not the message he had received from Hiram.

Jack Stewart sat back on the worn couch, his thoughts racing after decoding the latest message from Corry Woods. He knew something was out of the ordinary when the header on the message indicated it must be decoded by the separate key list carried only by Jack. It also meant the message was "eyes only" for Jack, a fact that Karl had noted without comment.

Sent from Baker Street, the message was signed "T" which meant it was from Noel Greene. It also told Jack that their presence had been compromised, which explained what Dmitri had seen on their trip into the city. Greene said they knew the mole on their end and were concerned that Ivanov might be working at crossed purposes. That didn't make sense to Jack, otherwise why would Dmitri have told them of seeing the two NKVD men? He thought only for a moment of Karl, his confidence in the man total. So someone was working against them from within Double OO. He should have been angry but he felt more puzzled than anything else. The close bonds formed over the last three years seemed impervious to any outside force. In addition each member had been vetted multiple times during that period. Who could it be?

There was a knock on the door which opened to reveal Karl.

"Is everything all right?"

"Apparently not. But it at least explains what Dmitri saw. Have him come in, we have work to do."

Dmitri entered the room carrying his MP-40.

"I hope you're not going to use that on us," Jack said wryly.

"Makes me feel better to have it close."

Karl and Dmitri sat down as Jack continued.

"Dmitri, it seems that you were quite right in your observations on the road. I've received a message that there is a mole at Corry Woods who has been relaying our position to the Soviets."

"Christ!" Karl said.

"What we don't know is their purpose. Are they trying to catch you or disrupt our mission?"

Dmitri's expression was grim but he offered no opinion.

"Does it matter?" Karl asked.

"Not really," Jack replied. "But if we want to succeed we have to take them out of the equation first."

The two other men nodded.

"Any suggestions?" Dmitri asked.

Jack stood up. "We need to set up an ambush and lead them into it."

"I agree," Karl said.

Dmitri nodded.

"We find a spot, make sure it fits our needs and then send the location to Corry Woods. They pass it on to the mole. Then we lay a trap for them."

Karl stood up, followed by Dmitri.

"Ready?" he asked.

As they filed out of the room, Karl asked, "Who is it?"

Jack shook his head, "They didn't tell me."

Chapter Fifteen

2 KM South of Trebnitz
17 April, 1945
1235 Hours

The long barrels of two 88mm artillery pieces pointed over several shallow trenches which ran diagonally across the slope. These new defensive lines had been hastily constructed as it became clear the Soviet advance would overrun the original defensive fortifications overlooking Seelow. Crouching behind very little cover, the German infantry waited for contact by the advancing Red Army units. An artillery barrage lasting almost 20 minutes had just ceased, telling the troops the enemy tanks and infantry would arrive shortly.

Albert Haselman looked at the men on either side of him. Filthy and unshaven, most carried only their weapons, packs discarded long ago during the retreat. Here and there an officer or non-com moved quietly from man to man offering a word of encouragement although everyone knew their situation was hopeless. This is what being a soldier is about, he thought. These men have nothing to fight for except each other now. But they would fight and they would die, not for Germany or National Socialism, but for their comrades. So I shall die here with them.

"Herr General, there's a truck being sent for you." Hauptman Erich Schrader crouched next to him.

Haselman turned to the young officer.

"Erich, I think we'll make a stand here." The General's eyes were bright as he smiled at his aide. "Put the wounded on the truck."

Schrader said nothing. Instead he handed an MP-38 machine pistol to the General. "I'll go find some more ammunition, sir."

Much of the German command structure had broken down during the initial retreat from the first set of defensive positions. The weight of the Soviet onslaught caught the German defenders like a tidal wave. Haselman had tried to coordinate the defensive effort north of the autobahn, but as units were overrun and decimated, the communication system broke down also. A direct hit on the General's radio truck by a Soviet artillery round finished his ability to issue orders.

Haselman lay against the front wall of the shallow trench looking down the narrow ravine through which the Soviet tanks must come. His thoughts returned to the First War and he remembered how he felt as a young Lieutenant waiting for his first attack. Then he had wanted to prove to himself and his men that he was a good soldier. Now he only wanted to die with dignity.

Schrader slid into the trench beside the General. In one hand he carried a canvas bag. "Extra ammunition, sir."

Firing erupted from a machine gun at the end of the trench.

Haselman looked down the slope seeing a single T-34 tank moving around an outcropping. There was no infantry in sight, but he knew they weren't far behind. "Keep your head down, Schrader," the General yelled. One of the 88's fired from behind them, hitting the T-34 which exploded in a blinding flash, the turret ripped open.

Troops were now visible, moving from behind the burning tank, seeking cover among the short trees and rocks on the sides of the

121

ravine. The German infantry began to fire as the enemy moved up the slope. So far, the Soviets were only firing their individual weapons, while the German heavy machine guns took a heavy toll as their targets moved within 200 meters of the first German trenches. The roar of fire increased as individual weapons joined the machine guns raking the advancing enemy troops.

Haselman checked that the clip was full, pulled the operating handle back to lock it, inserted the clip and released the handle. The weapon felt good in his hands after so much time behind a desk. Raising up he saw two Russians running low across the muddy road heading for a large rock. He squeezed the trigger aiming low while leading the first man. Both men stumbled and rolled as the General's bullets found their mark. Behind him the second 88 fired at a Russian tank, coming around the left side of the first burning tank. He could see at least a hundred Russian soldiers moving toward their position, which had less than forty Germans.

Beside him, Hauptman Schrader fired his MP-38, but it was becoming clear the Soviets had many more men coming through the gap at the bottom of the ravine.

"Grenades, Schrader, do we have grenades?"

"Yes, si......."

Haselman turned to see Erich Schrader on his knees, the left side of his face gone. Slowly the young man fell backwards against the back wall of the trench, rolling sideways into the mud. The terrible memories of the First War came back as if it were yesterday. He reached for another clip as he began to hear the cries of the attacking Russians. Looking over the lip of the trench, he saw a dozen soldiers, clad in the ugly brown of the Red Army making their way toward him. He felt very calm.

Willy looked down the corridor, confirming it was empty. Stepping into the small alcove, he found the desk outside Bormann's office empty also, Fraulein Krüger in bed many hours ago. He was counting on Bormann's reputation as a night owl, a habit the minister had developed in response to Hitler's unusual working hours. Light streamed from under the door. Willy knocked sharply.

"Come in," was the muffled response from within.

Bormann sat in low easy chair to one side of his desk. Very uncharacteristically his tie was loosened and collar open.

"Yes, Major, what do you want?"

Willy took a deep breath.

"Herr Minister, I must talk with you." Willy stood there awkwardly, seeing the impatient look on Bormann's face.

"Well, go ahead."

"Sir, I have been told you enjoy classical music."

Bormann said nothing but stood up and walked behind his desk.

"Sit down, Major." He indicated the chair he had just vacated.

"There are only a few pieces I truly enjoy," he said as he sat down behind his desk.

Willy hesitated for a moment then said, "Perhaps one of them might be Carl Bach's Symphony in G."

Bormann's eyes widened slightly. "Where did you hear that?"

"From a group of men I met with recently," Willy said, knowing the die had now been cast.

"And where are these men now?" Bormann asked slowly.

"Very near, Herr Minister."

"And why exactly are they here?"

123

"To take you out of Berlin."

Willy's words, though spoken quietly, seemed to echo around the small office. He was now fully committed regardless of the consequences.

"They have a way to get me out?"

"Yes, sir. The team has an aircraft on standby. They need to know when you can leave the bunker."

Bormann sat back and exhaled.

"When do you need to know?"

The response surprised Willy. Wouldn't he want to leave immediately? They hadn't discussed this at the lake, but he decided to take the initiative.

"Right away, Here Minister. The situation around Berlin will make leaving by aircraft more difficult as each day passes."

Bormann nodded as if he was considering all options.

"Does anyone else in the bunker know of this?"

"No, sir."

The ring was closing around the capitol and Martin Bormann knew it. At the same time he knew that the instant his absence was noted by Adolph Hitler, there would be a manhunt initiated by the dictator. The Fuhrer viewed loyalty as the highest virtue. Any betrayal would be handled swiftly and with lethality.

"I need to know the last day they think this plan is feasible. The timing will be critical for me. What can you tell me about the group?"

Willy wondered how the man would respond to his answer, but told him exactly what he had encountered in the little cottage by the lake.

"An American, a German and a Russian all working for the British Secret Service? This is hard to believe."

"Sir, I am simply telling you what I found. The men seem very capable. The German, Dietrich was one of Himmler's most successful commandos earlier in the war."

"My God," he said under his breath. But Martin Bormann knew this was going to be his only chance to escape certain death, either in the rubble of Berlin or in a Russian cell.

"Find out the last day we can do this and I'll make the appropriate arrangements."

Willy stood up.

"Major."

"Sir?"

"We are both in great danger. You must exercise the utmost caution if this is to succeed."

"I am very aware of that, Herr Minister."

Willy closed the door behind him and closed his eyes for one moment trying to compose himself. It seemed like events were taking control of him and that was a very uncomfortable feeling. He turned into the corridor toward the communication center. How was he going to get out of the bunker again without drawing Mueller's attention to him? If Sergeant Talbe was in the evening guard rotation he might be able to slip out after dark tonight.

"Herr, Major."

Turning, Willy saw Standartenfuhrer Heinz Muller walking behind him in the brightly lit corridor. How long had he been there? Did he see him come out of Bormann's office? Willy's heart pounded in his chest knowing this could go badly.

"Sir?"

"You're up late. I hope nothing is wrong." Mueller smiled slightly, the tone of his voice hard to read.

"I wanted to check the recent message traffic."

"Very good idea I would think. It would seem to me that keeping our leaders informed at a time like this is critical."

What was this man looking for, Willy wondered.

"Quite right, Herr Standartenfuhrer."

"And I know the Fuhrer and Minister Bormann always work late into the night."

"Yes, sir, that is correct."

"Very well, I don't want to keep you from doing your duty."

Willy turned and began to walk toward the communication center. Mueller suspects something, he thought.

Chapter Sixteen

Lubyanka Prison
Moscow
April 18, 1945

"Volkonsky's team missed the British at the first location," Konstantin Rostov read from a notepad. We have subsequently received the new position of the MI-6 team from Oscar and have transmitted that to our people."

Lavrenty Beria listened quietly, his arms folded on his chest.

Rostov continued, "We expect they will make a move sometime in the next twelve hours."

"And all we know is that they are trying to get someone out of the city?"

"Yes, sir."

"I want them to take those people alive. We need to find out what is so important that made Churchill send this team into Berlin now. I suspect there are things we could find out that might alter the future balance of power."

"It might be difficult to extricate the team once they have prisoners," Rostov offered.

"I don't give a damn! I want those men alive. They're no good to me dead. If our team needs to dig in and wait for our

Army to take Berlin, so be it. Make sure both Volkonsky and Malenkov understand that."

"Yes, sir," Rostov replied, knowing that it was going to be difficult to contact the team. They might already be on their way into Berlin.

"If you'll excuse me, sir, I'll send a message to the team."

After Rostov had left, Beria got up and began to pace his office. How much did he tell Stalin before the fact? He would gain credit for knowing about and sending his team after the British. But what if they were unsuccessful? This British team would be the best they had. While Volkonsky and Malenkov were good, it was always a gamble in this dark world of secret operations. No, he would wait until he had success to report to Stalin.

He continued to review his options. This might be good time to think about pulling Oscar out of England. The potential compromise during this operation might limit his future usefulness. Surely the British have been re-examining all of their people as the war draws to a close and you could never be sure what thread they might pull. While Oscar had been a key source of knowledge, there were two new spies that had now been supplying a much steadier stream of information to Rostov. Or perhaps he left Oscar in place until the British discovered him. Would having him in Moscow allow a debrief that would be more valuable than leaving him in place? Beria cared little for his agents beyond their use to him. If Oscar ended up at the end of a rope on a British gallows it would only show the world how treacherous the Anglo Saxon race was.

He looked at the clock. It was past mid-day, perhaps a stiff drink was in order.

Phillip Kent was angry and scared. The recent orders from Moscow had made him violate several rules that he knew raised the chance he might be discovered. Some day he would find out what was the urgency in this particular case. Now he had to ask himself why twice in the last two days he had seen what appeared to be men watching him. At his last meeting with Eva and then again this morning outside his house there had been a man sitting in an automobile reading a newspaper.

For a senior member of MI-5 to be under any type of shadowing, there must be someone in the government with strong evidence, if this was official. Or could the Soviets be shadowing him? If so what did that mean? If it was the British, what did they know? How could they have connected the recent events unless they had already suspected him? The thought ran a cold shiver through him. Suddenly the British security organization didn't seem so inept. Was it finally time for him to leave England? He knew some day he would have to flee, he never thought it would be so soon.

If he was to stay, he could only do it with one condition, Eva Papenhausen must not be around. She would be a constant threat to him. At some point she might have an attack of conscience and throw herself on the mercy of Noel Greene. Until this point her desire to remain close to Karl Dietrich had kept her from losing her head. But Eva had too much character to overcome her conscience forever.

He remembered back to their first very fateful meeting. Normally Kent did not get involved in field activities. But when his operative had told him there was a German woman who had come ashore, he was very intrigued. He didn't know then that she had fled Germany pretending to want to work for the Nazis when in fact all she wanted was to escape their regime. She'd apparently already intended to turn herself in and hope for leniency. All of this came to light later. But on that fateful night, she had panicked and killed Sydney Brown at the meeting place when he told her she would have to be a double agent. She hadn't intended to betray her country but simply turn herself in expecting to be arrested and held. When Kent discovered her with Brown's body he knew the potential. It was at that time Eva had begun to actively work for MI-5 under threat of Kent exposing her murder of Brown. Although she had over time realized that working for the British against the Nazis was what she wanted, Kent kept the threat of a murder charge over her head.

Now he knew that if he was to survive, she must not.

Sergeant Manfred Richter knelt down behind what remained of an 88mm artillery piece. His battalion had been fighting since earlier in the day to stop a Soviet push up the ravine. The savage fighting had only ended when three German Tiger tanks had made their way to the top of the slope and began to decimate the Soviet armor. It now appeared the Soviet infantry had withdrawn. The burning hulks of seven T-34's still smoldered, a dark ugly smoke rising from the wrecked vehicles.

Richter didn't know if he could move another step. He felt like his body was shutting down after the stress of the day's fighting. A veteran of two years in Russia, he had felt this way before and knew it would pass. But to what purpose he asked himself. The enemy never stops coming. More men and tanks. It seemed that no matter what the Wermacht tried, the Red Army overcame it and pressed forward.

He reached into his filthy tunic and found his last pack of Junos. Sitting back against an upturned stump he lit the cigarette, drawing the smoke into his lungs. Now if I just had a beer, he thought.

"Sergeant, come quick," Corporal Heinz Lentz said breathlessly. "We found a general and he's alive."

Sergei Volkonsky had just spent the last hour inspecting the building identified in Moscow's last transmission as the location of the British team. Relatively undamaged, the four story brick building appeared to be an apartment building over a small clothing store. The message had indicated the British were in apartment 201.

This neighborhood appeared to have suffered much more damage from bombing than the surrounding area and there were few civilian to be seen in the streets. Walking around the corner of a gutted building, he saw Gregori coming toward him. Malenkov's face gave no clue to his thoughts.

"There are two access points, the main entrance and a single door on the back alley. Looking through the window, the store appears abandoned, but you can see a stairway leading up to the second floor."

Sergei nodded. "I saw the same thing. Also I'm surprised there aren't many civilians in the area, which seems strange."

"Difficult to say," Malenkov said. "Could be some police or army restriction. I wouldn't worry too much about that, it makes our job easier."

The two men walked down the street toward the covered truck which contained the rest of the team. Only Sergeant Ruess remained with the Kubelwagen parked in a small alley off the main street.

They continued to observe every detail as they approached the truck.

Pulling himself up on the back of the truck, he pushed through the canvas flap and came face to face with Captain Kulyagin holding an MP-40 on him.

"Relax, Captain."

Malenkov followed him.

The sun had now begun to set and Sergei turned on a flashlight. "Here, hold this," he said to Kulyagin.

Under the pale light, he spread a chart with the map side down. Taking a pencil he began to sketch the street pattern, their current location and the entrance points on the target building.

"Everyone look at this," Volkonsky said. The commandos squeezed close around the circle of light. Twenty minutes later they began to slip out the back of the truck into the now dark street.

Karl Dietrich rubbed his eyes, the strain and fatigue beginning to catch up with him. Behind him Dmitri Ivanov lay back on a threadbare couch, his breathing regular. Karl had begun to like the gruff Russian and appreciated his ability to sleep anywhere. Not very talkative, there was a quiet strength about Dmitri that told anyone he was not a man to be crossed.

Next to him a set of binoculars lay on the table, useless now in the dark but earlier they had allowed Dmitri to confirm the NKVD was staking out the building across the street. Only four blocks from their real location, Jack and Karl had found a building which was deserted but almost undamaged. Their vantage point across the street was in the third floor of a severely damaged building that had also been deserted. Though temped by the appearance of the two men he recognized, Dmitri agreed that they would be dealing with the unknown if they tried to take them out on the street. They also would not know how many other members of the Russian team were in the area and possible covering the two agent's backs. Karl decided to stick with their original plan.

The street below was very dark but Karl spotted several men moving down the street toward number 23. He could tell by the way the group moved they were highly trained and moving with a purpose.

He shook Ivanov's foot. "Dmitri, wake up."

The Russian sat up, quickly rubbing his face and moving to the window.

"Down there," he said nodding toward the far side of the road. Four men moved quickly, several paces between each man. They appeared to be carrying weapons at the ready.

Moving to the main entrance, two men went to each side, hesitated momentarily then forced the door open.

"So there's at least four of them," Karl said quietly.

The men disappeared into the darkened shop interior. Karl imagined then moving cautiously up the stairs, weapons trained into the darkness. They would be very quiet, counting on surprise to take the British team unaware. Dmitri sat next to Karl saying nothing. This would be hard for him, Karl thought. But there's no other way.

A flash from within the darkened building preceded the loud explosion and flying glass as the windows on the second floor burst out in a thousand pieces.

"Let's go," Karl said.

Moving rapidly down the Hessenstrasse, Sergei Volkonsky's mind raced. At his side, Gregori Malenkov said nothing. They both understood they must get out of the area.

Sergeant Ruess watched the two men get into the Kubelwagen, looking to Volkonsky for orders.

"Drive. Go east but not fast. We don't want to attract any attention."

"It seems the game has become much different than we thought," Malenkov said, staring straight ahead.

"A set up, a damned set up," Volkonsky said angrily. "So much for Moscow's information. We've been played my friend. The question is who's playing with whom?"

Watching the darkened buildings move past, Volkonsky thought back to his meeting with Kalinin. While he trusted Rostov, perhaps the British had turned the agent and planted bad information. But how did they know there was an NKVD team in Berlin? Is Kalinin playing games or could Beria be up to something? He felt very unsettled as they drove back to their safe house. The message to Moscow must be thought out very carefully he told himself. Should he report the loss of the commandos or would that fact make its way to the British. Perhaps the MI-6 team thinks they took out the entire team with their booby trap. That would leave the two of us to stay after Ivanov. But where to begin? What had started out as a reasonable situation had now turned into looking for a needle in a haystack. But how could they trust anything from Moscow now?

Chapter Seventeen

KurfendamStrasse
Berlin
18 April, 1945
2015 Hours

"Four taken out, no question about it," Karl said as he wiped his face with a towel. "We watched them enter the building and the force of the explosion gutted the entire second floor. If anyone survived they had to be severely wounded. If there were more members of the team, I don't think they'd be willing to crawl through the rubble and take a chance of being discovered by rescue workers."

"You're probably right. Now we have to push getting Bormann out of here before anything else happens. We have to find out if the Major made contact with him."

Karl nodded. "Every day this drags out, the odds against us mount."

"Sergeant, you visited Major Haselman in the bunker."

"Yes, sir. I brought word from the General."

Jack looked at Karl. "We need to force the issue."

"I agree," Karl said.

"Sergeant, I need you to go to the bunker tonight. Use the same story that you are bringing word to Major Haselman from his father."

Hoffman stood up and began fastening the top buttons on his tunic.

"Once inside we need you to find out what's going on from the Major. Can you do that?"

"Yes, sir, I'll do my best." His voice told them all that he would die if needed.

Jack went on, "Try to be back here by midnight if possible. We must know their best estimate on when we can move. Also find out if there are any unusual security arrangements we need to know about."

The Sergeant nodded in acknowledgement as Jack went on, "Can you go on foot? I'd like to save the vehicle for the actual move."

"It's only a short walk," Hoffman said.

"All right then, on your way."

Ten minutes after the Sergeant left for the bunker, a short transmission was sent to Corry Woods.

The two men sat behind the closed door of Haselman's office. Willy didn't want Mueller seeing the Sergeant and asking any questions.

Have you heard anything from my father?" Willy asked Sergeant Hoffman.

"No, sir, not since early on the 16th when I left to meet the team."

136

Willy had read the operations reports which described the fierce fighting on the west side of the Oder. He knew his father would not give up the fight even though at this point it was clearly hopeless. Now he must try to put his father out of his mind.

"Tell me what has been happening,"

The Sergeant described their move into the city, the enemy agents they spotted on the road and the booby trap the British sprang on the Russians.

My God, Willy thought, there is so much happening that I don't understand. His ordered world was falling apart and now he realized he must do whatever was necessary to fulfill his last promise to his father.

"Sir, they said they must know the soonest that you can bring Herr Bormann out of the bunker. The Russian advance is threatening their plan."

Willy thought for a moment.

"Stay here. I'll be back shortly."

The light under Bormann's door was on. Willy knocked and opened the inner door after passing the secretary's empty desk.

Bormann looked up from the desk. Tonight there were no papers in front of him, only a bottle of wine and a single glass.

"Herr Major, do come in," Bormann said, his words slurred slightly.

Willy closed the door and walked to the desk.

"Sir, we must talk. I've had word from the British."

Bormann looked at him for a moment as if the words meant nothing to him.

"Yes, of course, the British. A miserable race you know. I never understood why the Fuhrer held them in such high regard." He added wine to his half full glass.

"They're ready to take you out of Berlin. But we must tell them when you can go. Time is running out. General Reymann's staff thinks they may only be able to hold the Russians for another week."

Taking a drink first, Bormann looked at Willy, his eyes now clear. "I know."

"What shall I tell them?"

The older man looked at his glass then drained the contents.

"Tell them I will leave when the Fuhrer is dead."

"And if that destroys their plans to get you out of the city?"

"Then I die in the city. But I will not leave the Fuhrer."

"He said what?" Jack found it hard to comprehend what Sergeant Hoffman had just told him.

The Sergeant repeated the message which Willy Haselman had given him.

"He's a fool," Karl said.

"What's that?" Dmitri Ivanov asked sleepily, rubbing his eyes.

"Bormann won't leave until Hitler is dead," Karl replied.

"Thoughts?" Jack asked his team.

"We can't do it," Karl said. "The Junkers probably has one chance to get into land and then get away. We can't expect them to react after the fact. Bormann needs to make a decision. Either he comes with us or stays to deal with the Russians."

Jack knew that the Russians must not get their hands on Bormann. Noel Greene had been very specific that capture by any country other than Great Britain must be avoided at all costs.

138

"What flexibility do you have?" Dmitri asked.

"None when it comes down to who ends up with Bormann," Jack said.

"Sergeant, is there some place we could move nearer to the bunker? As the Russians close in, we may have to fall back to the bunker and wait for him to come out. Then we'll figure out how to get out of the city without using an aircraft."

"Dmitri, you may still be the key to this operation. If we have to get through the Russian checkpoints, it will take someone who knows their system."

How many NKVD personnel would be with the front line troops as they pushed into the capitol, Dmitri wondered? Certainly there would be some and perhaps with the importance of closing the net, Moscow might have augmented the field units. The thought made him turn cold. Not only was he well known within the NKVD, Dmitri knew that Beria would send his picture sent out to every military police detachment in the Red Army.

"We're quickly losing the air option," Jack went on. "I'd be willing to have them land at Tempelhof but it may be in Russian hands in the near future. Perhaps we should just plan on moving west after we get Bormann and make our way to the American lines."

"It still has to be by air," Karl said. "Trying to get a well known Nazi across that much territory would be a fool's errand. Instead we find somewhere outside the city where they can land. On the ground minimum time, and at dusk we're back over the lines before anyone can react."

Jack nodded. "I agree. But we'll still need Dmitri to run interference for us. This city will be crawling with troops and security service."

"Sir, if I might suggest?" Sergeant Hoffman asked tentatively.

"Please do, Sergeant, we're running out of ideas."

The Sergeant continued, "There is a large area about 25 kilometers west of the city where the Luftwaffe built a temporary landing field. I drove the General there several times. It's not built up at all but the landing area is large and safe."

"Where?" Karl asked.

"South off the main road from Rohrbeck, perhaps 5 or 6 kilometers."

Karl unfolded a map and scanned it for a moment.

"Here it is."

Jack and Dmitri leaned over to see the chart.

"That could work. We move closer to the bunker, grab Bormann when we can and make our way to Rohrbeck," Jack said.

Dmitri asked, "What happens if the area is already held by the Red Army?"

Jack smiled. "That's where you come in." Karl looked at his two team mates with skepticism. "There's nothing easy about this. Let's figure out what we need to pull it off."

"Divine intervention, my German friend," Jack laughed. "I'm just glad God's on our side."

Eva Papenhausen walked slowly down the first floor corridor in the east wing toward the mission support room. For the middle of the morning it was remarkably quiet. Pam Thompson would be on watch for the next hour and a half. But Eva had to try and find out the location of the team right away. She'd never seen Kent as angry and insistent as earlier this morning when they'd met in the village. He told her that he needed to know exactly where the three men were and he needed to know right now.

"Hello, Pam," she said walking into the room.

Pam glanced up. "There you are. I looked for you earlier but Anna said you'd gone into the village."

Eva sat down at a table covered with maps. "I promised to pick up a shawl Mrs. Morton knitted for Karl."

"Did you get it?"

She nodded. "It's very pretty. She does wonderful work."

"Read this message. It was decoded right after you went off shift."

Eva opened the red folder and began to read as she sat down opposite Pam. As she read the message over again the terrible reality hit her like a hammer.

"They're headed for the lion's den," Pam added.

"Lion's den?" Eva asked, sounding mildly confused.

"The bunker," Pam said. "They're going to work their way to the Health Ministry. It's only a block away from the bunker and apparently deserted. They can hold out there until they can find the target."

Eva had the answer to her question.

Chapter Eighteen

Maidstone, Kent
April 1945

Eva slowed the car, searching for the first driveway past the bridge. She had never been to this location before. It wasn't one of the normal MI-5 safe houses. Turning into the narrow road, there were hedges on both sides just as Kent had described. They were to meet in the small cottage at the end of the driveway.

The drive from Corry Woods to Maidstone had taken a little more than an hour. Eva had departed when her shift ended at 1800 hours. She hadn't bothered to change and still wore her slacks and sweater from this morning. But she had to find Kent. That was all that was important. For the first time since he had come back into her life, she wasn't hesitant to see him. It gave her a sense of power which helped to calm her nerves.

Ahead she could see the cottage. Light streamed from two small windows illuminating a small Ford parked at the front door. Eva slowed and stopped behind the other car, pausing for a moment before she turned off the ignition. One last check of her purse and she got out of the car. Slowly closing the door she stopped and listened for any sounds that might indicate anyone was close by. It was eerily quiet and it gave her more confidence as she stepped up on the porch and knocked on the door.

"Hello, Eva. Right on time. Do come in."

She didn't reply as she pushed past Kent into the small living room.

"You seem a bit put off this evening. Sit down." Kent followed her into the room.

She walked over to a small couch and sat at the end, her purse on her lap.

"Did you get the information?" he asked, sitting down in a small chair across from the couch.

"Phillip, who are you working for?"

He looked at her with mild surprise then replied, "What a strange question."

"Someone made an attempt on our team. The only one outside of our group who had any information about their specific location was you."

"That is a very interesting conclusion. But there isn't a shred of truth in it." He tried to remain relaxed, but he knew if she had told anyone in MI-6 of his activities he was in immediate danger.

"Isn't it a strange coincident that you showed up at Corry Woods when you did, right before this mission?"

"As you say, merely a coincidence."

143

"Didn't you always teach me that you didn't believe in coincidences?" Eva looked down and unlatched the flap on her purse, reaching inside.

"Don't do that if you want to live a minute longer," Kent said.

Eva looked across to the room to see a pistol pointed at her.

"Put your purse of the floor…slowly."

Kent stood up, keeping the pistol leveled at Eva's chest. He walked over and kicked her purse to the side of the room.

"You stupid woman. If you would have just left things alone, we could have both gone about our business. Now you've pushed me into a corner. You will regret that."

Despite the terrible danger, Eva felt calm. Whether she found out the truth or not, this man would no longer use her to get at Karl.

The Ford sedan pulled out on the main road, the slotted headlights swinging in a horizontal arc against the opposite fence as it accelerated south on Sutton Road.

One minute later Phil Hatcher pulled out on the road heading south. He was glad there was some moonlight, his headlights were off.

Four days later, Phillip Kent looked up from his paper to see the red light on his private line flashing. Only a select few in government possessed the number which allowed discreet discussions without the normal recording protocol for public calls into MI-5.

"Kent here."

"Phillip, it's Noel Greene."

"Hello, Noel. What can I do for you?"

"I'm afraid I have some rather bad news."

"Go ahead," Kent said cautiously

"It's Eva. A beach patrol found her body washed up near Hastings."

"Oh my God," Kent said. "Do we know what happened?"

"Too early to tell. A local police inspector in Hastings thought she'd been in the water for at least a week."

"Noel, I'm devastated. She was such a wonderful woman."

"You're right. The group at Corry Woods is taking it rather badly. I suspect it had something to do with the Germans."

"The Germans, yes. Is there anything that MI-5 can do to assist you or the police?"

"Not right now. I'm sure that we'll be able to turn something up. But I'll let you know."

Noel Greene placed the phone on the receiver and sat back in his chair.

Across from him Phil Hatcher returned a second handset to its cradle.

"The bastard," Greene said, the anger vivid in his eyes.

Phil said nothing, his thoughts on that night when he had dropped back while following the Ford as they passed through High Halden. South of town he immediately knew that Kent had given him the slip. Had the traitor known he was there or was it just bad luck? Phil knew he would never forgive himself for letting Eva down.

"How do we move on this?"

Greene shook his head. "There's no easy way. There may be other plants in MI-5. Do we try to gather more evidence or just put Kent behind bars awaiting the hang man?"

"If he suspects anything, he might run. I'm sure the Soviets have set up some kind of contingency plan."

145

"No question. But if we don't alert him, we may be able to keep unraveling his network before taking down the whole thing."

Phil stood up and walked to the window. "That will take the kind of manpower we don't have readily available. And if we bring in too many people the chances of alerting Kent go up."

"Perhaps he's working alone," Greene asked.

"In which case we have no idea when he might run."

"I'll have to brief the Prime Minister. Not only could this affect the mission, it could blow up in his face at exactly the wrong time."

When Hatcher had left, Greene reached for the intercom and asked that his car be brought around. He would see what he might do to put a cork back in this bottle.

Chapter Nineteen

The Reich Health Ministry
Berlin
30 April, 1945

Rapid explosions reverberated in the distance. The bombardment by the Soviets had been almost non-stop since the team had positioned themselves in the abandoned ministry. Jack looked across at his comrades sleeping on the floor of the corner room they had used as their base of operations for the last week. While spending most of their time within the thick stone walls of the ministry, they had also conducted a thorough reconnaissance of the area surrounding the bunker and ministry. Blending in with the military units setting up defensive positions had proved to be easy in the constant confusion created by the Soviet artillery.

Another string of explosions echoed against the walls, the detonations closer than the last. Katusha rockets, Jack thought. The rapid crashes didn't sound like the heavy Soviet artillery that had been pounding the city for the last four days. Assault units of the Red Army were now less than two kilometers from the bunker. The world outside the ministry had taken on an unreal quality. The smoke and dust from bursting shells created a changing landscape where people were only seen rushing for cover. Fires throughout the city created a low hanging dark cloud that even the wind couldn't dissipate.

Karl coughed then coughed again. Slowly he sat up and rubbed his eyes.

"What time is it?"

"A little before two. You slept almost an hour," Jack replied.

"Anything happening?"

"Nothing close. The artillery's gotten heavier in the last hour."

Karl nodded. "They're getting ready for a push."

"And I would just as soon not be here when the red horde arrives."

"Then we have to force the issue," Karl said.

"We'll send the Sergeant back in to contact Haselman. This time an ultimatum, leave now or you're on your own. The Sergeant should be back shortly."

Sergeant Hoffman returned from his search for rations with a haversack thrown over his shoulder.

"All I could find was some of the new German "K-rations."

Placing the bag on a small table, he opened it and pulled out a small cardboard box, offering it to Jack.

"Thank you, Sergeant." Hoffman had been procuring their daily rations from what he could find or buy in the streets. The team still had their emergency rations but were saving them.

Karl took a box from the Sergeant and sat down on the couch.

"Let him sleep," Jack said looking at Dmitri fast asleep on a blanket.

"No wonder Germany is losing the war," Karl said after taking a bite from a small food bar. "This is terrible."

Jack tentatively bit a piece off the end of a similar bar.

"They are fruit bars, sir," The Sergeant said in explanation.

Continuing to chew, Jack smiled thinly at Sergeant Hoffman. "Very interesting taste."

"The crackers are edible," Karl said as he threw the box next to his blanket. "Now we just need cheese and some beer."

"Sergeant, I know you just got back, but we must get a message to Major Haselman. Do you think you can get to the bunker?"

Hoffman nodded. "Yes, sir. There are several ways from here that I can take, most of which are underground through the shelter system for the Reichschancellery."

Karl looked surprised. "I would have thought most of the bureaucrats would have fled this area by now."

"They have, sir. The shelter areas are being used as hospital wards for the injured from the front."

"You can leave as soon as we give you the message to pass to the Major. It is very critical this message get through as soon as possible."

"Jack, I think it makes sense for me to go with the Sergeant."

As he started to object, Jack stopped himself. Karl was right. Getting the message to Haselman was too important. At least they would know Hoffman made it to the bunker. "I agree."

The two men stooped low and moved down the dirty concrete steps into an arched tunnel. Two years on the Eastern Front should have prepared Karl for the stench that came from the dimly lit corridor. A mixture of odors combining urine, feces, rotting flesh and dirty bodies greeted them.

Karl followed the Sergeant into a wide passageway with cots against the brick walls. Moisture from the walls ran down in small rivulets to the muddy floor. It looked to Karl like most of the inhabitants of the shelter were wounded soldiers. Several men wearing the red crosses of medical orderlies tended the injured men. Christ, Karl thought, this is what Germany has come to…broken men hiding in caves.

"This way, sir." Hoffman turned into a larger corridor that ran at right angles to the first passage.

Stepping over men lying on the floor, Karl saw filthy bandages that had not been changed recently. Some of the injuries appeared to have only field dressings, while other had the appearance of post-surgical care. Most of those bandages covered stumps of amputated arms and legs.

A young soldier with a bloody bandage covering the left side of his face sobbed as they passed. The men lying on the filthy floor were deathly quiet, staring straight ahead, waiting for the end. What would happen to these men when the Russians took the city? In the distance Karl heard artillery explosions. The Red Army would not be long.

Hoffman ducked to move under a large rusty pipe running across the top of the corridor. "Watch your head."

Karl saw the Sergeant stop and stare at a man sitting on the concrete floor, his back against the slimy brick wall.

Kneeling down next to the man, Hoffman leaned forward to get a closer look at the wounded soldier.

"Do you know him?"

"Sir, it's the General," Hoffman managed to say, his voice trembling with emotion.

"What?" Karl snapped.

"General......General," the Sergeant said, now on his knees next to a man wearing a sergeant's tunic.

"Are you sure," Karl asked. The light was dim and the man had dirt and blood covering the left side of his face.

Ignoring the question, Hoffman gently shook the man's arm. "Herr General, it's Hoffman."

The man slowly opened his eyes but continued staring straight ahead. He made no attempt to look at the Sergeant.

Karl knelt down and looked closely at the man. Sergeant Hoffman was right, it was Albert Haselman. Karl had last seen him over two years ago in Russia, but there was no question. The General had been wounded in the left side of his head. His scalp, matted with dried blood, looked black, contrasting with his gray hair.

"General, it's me, Hoffman." The Sergeant's voice was urgent. He unbuttoned the filthy uniform and gently checked the General's torso for additional wounds. He turned to Karl. "What should we do?"

"Sergeant."

Both men turned to look at the General who now was staring directly at Hoffman. There was recognition in his eyes.

"Yes, sir. I'm here."

Haselman took a deep breath and closed his eyes.

"Where are we?" he asked, his voice soft.

"Berlin, sir. Near the Reichschancellery."

Behind them a man yelled, his voice full of fear. Karl turned and saw two orderlies holding the man down for a doctor.

151

"What happened? How did I get here," the General asked, his eyes remaining closed.

Karl knew what he had to do. "Stay here with him."

"Yes, sir," the Sergeant answered without taking his eyes off the General.

Every hour in the bunker had become more surreal to Willy. As the word of the Russian advance trickled in from reporting stations, he had seen every emotion from fear to resignation. The fabric of the German leadership was unraveling as he watched. The constant coming and going of aides and messengers had all but ceased. The odor of tobacco, forbidden by Hitler, now mingled with the foul odors from backed up sewers and unwashed bodies. In many rooms, hoarded alcohol had appeared and was flowing freely. Messages into the communication center were sporadic and told a tale of the continuing surrender of German units. And still Bormann went about his daily duties as if it was just another day in the Fuhrer's schedule.

But Willy could sense a difference in the man. His normal solicitousness had been replaced by clipped conversations and brusque orders to those around him. When would he finally admit that his pledge to remain with Hitler was foolish? Until it was too late to escape?

Willy felt the pull of duty. But when did remaining in the bunker become pointless? Do we all stay here waiting for explosives to be pitched down from above? He asked himself. To die in this stinking concrete coffin? Germany was beaten. There was nothing anyone could do to prevent a victory by their enemies.

"Sir?"

Drawn from his thoughts he turned to see Sergeant Talbe in the doorway.

"Hello, Sergeant."

"This man is here to see you," Talbe said, stepping aside for Dieter Hoffman to enter.

Willy grabbed Hoffman by the shoulders. "I'm glad to see you in one piece. Here, sit down."

"Sergeant Talbe, thank you. If you could leave us?"

"Certainly, Herr Major." Talbe hesitated then said, "Sir, call me if you need anything."

Willy looked at the Sergeant who nodded slightly as he closed the door.

"What's happening?" he asked Hoffman.

The man hesitated. "Sir, your father has been wounded. We found him in the shelter near the Reichschancellery."

Grabbing Hoffman's arm, Willy asked, "How is he?"

"I don't know. The British team took him back to their hideout in the Health Ministry. He's been wounded in the head, but seemed to be coming around when I left to come here."

"When was that?"

"No more than an hour ago," Hoffman replied. "Sir, they told me to pass a message to you. You must leave now or the plan has no chance of success."

"Who is watching my father?"

Hoffman wiped his dirty face. "When I left him to come here, Colonel Dietrich and Commander Stewart were with him."

Willy thought about his father, the true warrior who had done his duty. Anger welled up within him. "Wait here."

A small group of very senior officers stood at the end of the central corridor which ran past the chart room. Willy saw Bormann standing with General Krebs, the two men talking quietly. He walked around Krebs, nodding at the senior officer and said to Bormann, "Sir, there are several messages on your desk. Perhaps you have time to review them now?"

"Major, can't you see we were talking?" Krebs asked, the irritation plain in his voice.

"It's fine, Herr General. I should only be a few minutes," Bormann said and turned for his office before Krebs could reply.

Willy swung the door shut as Bormann turned around, his eyes red and showing the strain of the last week.

"There are no messages," he said sitting down at his desk.

"No, sir. I have a message from the British. You must leave now or the plan is off."

Bormann looked at Willy, almost as if he hadn't heard.

"Did you hear me?"

"There are details which I must see to for the transition of power to Doenitz. We are selecting new ministers who are not in Berlin and will be able to take over when the city falls."

"You're living in a make believe world. Germany's new government will not be run by Germans. We are a defeated people."

Anger flared in Martin Bormann's eyes. "I should have you shot for saying that.

Willy stared back at him hard, his anger just in check. "I am leaving to go to my father. He has been wounded but lives. Do what you must, but I will leave in fifteen minutes. If you want to go with me I will take you to the British team." He turned and left the office without another word.

Bormann sat at his desk, his eyes fixed on the closed door.

Albert Haselman lay back on the folded blankets, a single cover over his chest. Karl knelt next to him working on his scalp, a small medical kit open on the floor.

"This does not look serious, Herr General," he said, carefully wiping a gauge pad on the wound. "Someone has already cleaned it and there doesn't seem to be any infection. I'll use some sulfa powder to be sure."

"Thank you."

"Is your headache still as bad?" Jack asked.

"The water helped," the General replied. His breathing was steady and voice stronger.

Karl finished wrapping a bandage around the General's head and leaned back. "I'm not a nurse, but I think that will do."

Jack carried over an open ration can with a spoon in it. He leaned down and said, "See if you can get this down."

The General hesitated then nodded.

One spoon at a time, Jack fed him, the only sound now the artillery in the distance.

"What is that?" the General asked after swallowing.

"Beef stew."

"Very good, thank you."

There were two quick knocks on the door and Dmitri, who had been on watch, appeared.

"Jack, the Sergeant's back."

Dieter Hoffman entered, followed by Willy Haselman.

Both men's eyes went to the General and Hoffman moved to one side for Willy to get to his father.

The General looked up at his son, saying nothing but extending his left hand.

Willy knelt down and took his father's hand.

Chapter Twenty

The Reich Health Ministry
Berlin
1 May, 1945

Jack kept watch on the interior courtyard of the ministry. The marble floor was covered with broken glass and debris from the last week of bombardment. Except for the occasional soldier or civilian, the deserted building sat in mute testimony to the destruction of the German state. Offices with burned files and broken furniture were all that remained of a bureaucracy that had controlled Europe for the last decade.

"All quiet?"

"Haven't seen anything but rats this morning," Jack replied.

Karl sat down next to him, stretching his legs out on the floor. "It's time to move."

"I know," Jack agreed. "But we still have the unfinished issue of Herr Bormann." He remembered Churchill's words. "......the Americans or the Russians must never talk to him."

"I think events are out of our control at this point."

Jack thought for a moment. "If Bormann is still in the bunker, we could make one last try for him."

Karl looked with surprise at his friend.

"I'm sure there's complete chaos by now. That might allow us a chance to get in and out."

"It might," Karl said with little enthusiasm.

Willy Haselman helped his father sit up against the wall.

"That's better," the General said, "My head has finally stopped aching."

"Here, drink some water."

It had been a quiet night for the small group. Sergeant Hoffman was able to find several cans of soup during his evening search. A small fire allowed them to produce a stew of sorts and all of them, including the General, had complimented the cook.

"Do we know what the situation is?"

Willy shook his head. "As of yesterday, the lines were holding. But everyone knew it was only a matter of time before the Russians pushed their way to the Reichschancellery."

"What do you know of their plans?" The General's voice had regained its old authority.

"Sergeant Hoffman told me they were going to try and get to Rohrbeck. Then an aircraft would pick them up."

"The Red Army might have something to say about that."

Willy nodded. Their prospects were not good.

158

Dmitri relieved Jack, who had remained talking with Karl.

"Still quiet."

Checking the action of his MP-40, Dmitri sat down and smiled at the two men.

"I think we are running out of quiet time."

"We are thinking of making one last try for Bormann. Then we head for Rohrbeck."

"Whatever we do, now is the time."

"We must try to get Bormann," Jack said to Willy. "If you brief us, Karl and I can try to get into the bunker. If we can talk to Bormann, that might be enough to get him to come with us."

The tall Major looked at Jack. He knew it made no sense to send these men to the bunker by themselves. If there was any way to get through to Bormann, Willy had the best chance. But he saw his father leaning against the wall with his eyes closed. How could he leave him?

Karl saw Willy glance at his father.

"Do you know the area around Rohrbeck?"

Willy looked surprised at the question.

"The RAF is going to try and pick us up from the landing field south of the town. I'll need you to help your father get to the rendezvous."

The words hit Willy like a hammer. Karl Dietrich was telling him to save his father from the Russians.

"But you will need me to get you into the bunker."

Karl smiled. "Leave it up to me."

Willy looked again at his father. "I'll go with you and we will get Bormann. Then we'll all go to Rohrbeck."

Fires burned throughout the shattered buildings surrounding the entrance to the bunker. A pall of oily smoke rose into the darkness. The bunker's SS security force was still in place although it appeared to Willy that there were far fewer troops manning the defensive positions next to the entrance. Beside the wide metal doors a small fire flared up casting deep shadows across the concrete bunker wall. Two SS troopers stood at relaxed attention, their machine pistols over their shoulders.

Leaning against the shadowed side of a long wall the three men watched the activity around the entrance to the bunker.

"Jack should stay here," Karl said. "I can convince Bormann if anyone can."

"Not true, my friend," Jack replied, not taking his eyes off the entrance. "He needs to see a British officer in person. If that doesn't convince him then nothing will."

Karl knew Jack made sense.

"Keep watch out here, and if we're not back in thirty minutes, then use your own judgment."

"Are you ready" Willy asked.

Jack nodded.

The two men moved casually toward the double door. The sentries didn't show any reaction. A group of three SS men stood to one side of the door. One of the men detached himself and walked to toward Willy. He looked hard at Willy then said, "Hello, Major."

Jack walked next to Willy trying to look bored.

"Herr Hauptman. It seems very quiet tonight."

The man said sarcastically. "Just give Ivan a few minutes."

They approached the door.

"How close are they?" Willy asked.

"Too close," the man said, leaving Willy to decide what he meant.

The two sentries glanced at them as they stepped through the doors.

Inside the concrete antechamber flickering electric lights showed the bunker's generators were still functioning.

Sergeant Talbe looked up in surprise.

"I didn't think I would see you again, Herr Major."

"What is happening?"

"It's like rats deserting a sinking ship. Since the Fuhrer died yesterday, they have been leaving constantly."

Hitler is dead, Willy thought. I should be happy, but it doesn't matter anymore he told himself.

"Is Bormann still here?"

Talbe nodded. "As far as I know."

Willy turned to Jack. "Let's go."

As they started to descend the stairs, a group of men at the bottom started up.

Willy motioned Jack back onto the landing to wait for the group to pass.

Martin Bormann exited the top step and almost ran into Willy.

"Herr Minister," Willy said in surprise.

The heavy set Bormann looked tired and anxious.

"Major, I looked for you," he said as two other men joined him in the guard chamber. "I was hoping we could work something out."

"I believe we can still do that," Willy said.

"You know Herr Axmann and Doctor Stumpfegger, I believe."

"Yes, sir. And this is Colonel Reinhard. I am sure I mentioned his special mission."

Bormann stared hard at Jack, his eyes intense. "Yes, of course." I am carrying a message from Goebbels to Doenitz. They are coming with me." He motioned to Axmann and Stumpfegger.

161

Willy tried to think. This was a twist they hadn't talked about. Axmann had been the leader of the Hitler Youth and Stumpfegger was Hitler's surgeon. Now it appeared they had joined with Bormann. How did that affect the Britisher's mission?

Karl saw a group of men emerge from the double doors and realized it was Jack and Willy Haselman. There were three other men with them. The group turned south walking toward Frederichstrasse. He waited as they walked past the trenches which protected the SS security troops. Karl decided to follow at a discrete distance until he figured out what was happening. As he moved from the shadow of the building, he froze. A single man appeared to be following Jack's group as it moved south. Karl waited a moment then followed the man.

Phillip Kent walked carefully down the alley off Whitside Street in Chelsea. He'd received a quick response to his emergency request for a meeting. This was extremely unusual, Kent could count on one hand the number of times he had met with a contact from the embassy in the last five years. But he needed answers now and would have to take the chance.

In the darkness he saw a sign attached to the brick wall. He took out a match to quickly confirm it said "Murphy Distributor's Ltd." Taking a deep breath, Kent slowly turned the doorknob. The latch opened and he swung the door open.

It was dark inside the door but there was enough light to see two rows of tables lining the room. Beyond the tables a door was partially open, the light of a candle providing the barest illumination. He walked to the door, pulling the small pistol from his coat pocket. Slowly

162

opening the door he saw a single man sitting at a wooden desk holding a lit cigarette in his left hand.

"Come in," he said, raising the cigarette to take a drag. The man noticed Kent's gun and said, "That is not necessary. This location is clean."

"I don't take chances," Kent said sitting down opposite the man who he recognized as Anatoly Krishkin. On the staff of the Soviet Embassy, now Kent knew that Krishkin was NKVD.

"Suit yourself," Krishkin said. "Now what do you want?"

"I think I have come under suspicion."

"Why do you say that?"

"Unless you're following me, someone else is and I'm afraid it's MI-6."

Krishkin crushed the cigarette out on the desk, the smoke rising into the darkness. "We have not been following you."

"So it must be the British. You need to tell Moscow it's time for me to come in."

Lighting another cigarette, he nodded. "I will pass on your request. I'm sure we can have an answer in short order. It will take several days to arrange something."

"Several days!" Kent was angry. "They could pick me up anytime."

"If they were going to pick you up, they would have already done so. Let us work on this. We know what we're doing. In the meantime, go about your daily routine. Don't do anything that would draw attention to yourself."

Kent felt frustrated. Something wasn't right and the Russian didn't seem to care. He knew what he must do.

"I'll leave a drop at Marleybone when I know something," Krishkin said, getting up and blowing the candle out.

"Fine."

Krishkin returned to the embassy by a circuitous route, not that he worried anyone was following him. Instead he wanted time to think. The NKVD station chief, Vladimir Popov, was waiting for him when he arrived.

Karl closed the distance with the group of men as they made their way down Frederichstrasse. Here and there people would appear, everyone on the move. Tracers arced across the river as the Soviet attack moved toward the Weidenhammer railroad bridge. Where are they going? Karl wondered. This route was taking them farther from the Health Ministry and closer to the Red Army.

Bormann ducked as an artillery round impacted a building next to the river. Two more explosions threw debris across the road, the small group taking cover behind a burned-out streetcar.

"I think this is a bad idea," Axmann said as they waited for the smoke to clear. "The Russians are down there," he said motioning toward the river.

"The Russians are everywhere, Herr Axmann," Willy said.

"Artur, you don't have to come with us. If you want to go another way, be my guest." Bormann sounded tired and angry.

The small Axmann looked around the group as another shell burst near the railroad bridge. "I'm going back the way we came. It might be easier to pass through the fighting to the south."

"Suit yourself, my friend."

A volley of machine gun fire crashed across the street as Axmann shook hand with his two companions.

"Good luck," Bormann said.

The former leader of a million Hitler Youth ran down the street, bent low to present a smaller target.

"Now what?" Bormann asked.

"We execute our plan," Jack said, speaking for the first time.

Doctor Stumpfegger looked at Jack in surprise, then to Bormann. "What is going on here?"

"Colonel Reinhard is with British Intelligence. They are going to get me out of Berlin. That's correct isn't it?"

"Yes, that's correct."

Stumpfegger looked stunned. "Bormann, how long has this been going on?"

"It doesn't matter. The only thing now is to get out of this city and away from the Russians."

From the near end of the streetcar, Heinz Mueller stepped into the light. He held a pistol leveled at the group.

"Collaboration with the enemy is punishable by death, Herr Minister."

He stepped closer, the pistol pointed directly at Martin Bormann.

"Don't move, or I will shoot," Mueller said, stopping five paces from Bormann. He looked at Willy who was standing next to Stumpfegger. "I knew there was something going on, Herr Major. It appears that both members of the Haselman family are traitors to Germany. Cripples and traitors who will not escape our fury."

Three shots rang out, pitching Heinz Mueller forward onto the street.

"Everyone freeze." Karl moved into the light, his MP-40 leveled at the group. "Jack, what's going on here?"

"I'm not sure. Major?"

165

Willy moved forward. "Heinz Mueller, one of Himmler's security agents."

"He followed you from the bunker," Karl said without emotion.

"Good timing," Jack said. Now let's get out of here."

"Where are you going?" Doctor Stumpfegger asked harshly.

"We're going to get out of this city," Jack said as he surveyed the nearest cross street which ran west. "You can come along if you like, otherwise you are free to go."

"I'll remain with you."

"We're heading for the Health Ministry," Jack told Karl.

"We can cut west from here and probably enter the shelters on the east side of the Chancellery."

"I know an entrance on that side," Willy said. "As long as the Russians aren't there."

"I'll take the lead," Karl said.

The group moved off into the smoke.

Lavrenty Beria sipped at the glass of bitter tea as he read the morning's intelligence summary.

There was a knock at the door and Kostantin Rostov entered. He walked to the desk and stood silently until Beria looked up.

"Did you bring me good news?"

"Actually no, Comrade Commissar."

Beria flipped the report closed. "Sit down."

Rostov hesitated then said, "We have received a message from London. Our deputy station chief met with Oscar. Oscar feels that the British suspect him. He is asking to be brought in."

"What do you think," Beria asked, expecting Rostov to recommend immediate rescue.

"There's something else. MI-6 thinks Oscar killed one of their agents to prevent her exposing him."

"Did he?"

"We think so," Rostov said.

"How do we know this?"

"Noel Greene arranged a meeting with Popov."

Beria knew Rostov maintained communications with Greene. The two men had met many years ago and developed a mutual respect. Their relationship had helped on several critical Soviet-British operations during the war.

"And?"

"They have a proposal."

Sergeant Hoffman pulled the large wood door closed and slid the locking bar in place. He turned and walked past the medium sized utility truck to the small door at the back of the makeshift garage. Resting on the floor was a jerry can. "I hope this is enough," he said aloud and picked up the container. Gasoline was almost impossible to obtain, but he had been able to find the small can, which was half full. He emptied it into the gas tank and replaced the cap.

Closing the small door, he slid a broken table in front to discourage entry. Now back to the Russian, he thought without enthusiasm. Sergeant Hoffman had maintained his distance from Dmitri. Perhaps it had been the time he spent on the Eastern Front or the propaganda about the Russians, but he had spoken to him very little over the last ten days.

Now it was only the Russian, the General and himself alone in the Ministry. He hoped the Major would be back soon.

"Did you find more fuel?" Dmitri asked.

"Not much, but it should get us to Rohrbeck."

167

Dmitri smiled. "I think Sergeants are the same in any army. If you need something, they will find it."

He actually sounds friendly, Hoffman thought. A Russian? Hoffman knelt down next to the General.

"He's been asleep for the last hour," Dmitri offered.

The Sergeant didn't disturb the General who continued to sleep soundly.

Chapter Twenty-One

East London
2 May, 1945

Phillip Kent finished his transformation by putting on large dark rimmed glasses and staring at himself in the mirror. His mustache had been shaved off and his normally light brown hair was now dark black. His identity card identified the bearer as Herbert P. Walker and Kent was the exact image of the man on the card. The result of a meticulous plan he had put in place over the last four years, Kent now had a valid identity complete with all necessary documentation. Using the capability of MI-5, he not only had a duplicate identity, but also an apartment in the east end of London where he intended to remain until the Soviet's could bring him in safely. Regardless of what Krishkin had told him, he was taking no chances that MI-6 was on to him. His disappearance would certainly give credence to any theories they might have at this point, but he was now invisible.

"We've got a bit of a problem, Dicky."

Closing the door, Dicky Thompson walked over to the large table where Terry Toms had a large map of Berlin spread out.

"Sir?"

"We just received the staging message for picking up Jack and his crew."

Dicky knew that every day the recovery was delayed, chances of success went down. At least now they could get busy.

Toms continued, "While we have the pickup point, we don't know who's in control on the ground."

"Germans or Russians?"

"Could be either. Right now there's fighting in the area. The Soviets should take control at some point, but we don't know when."

"How do we determine that?" Dicky asked.

"Jack has to get to the landing zone and let us know."

"Where's the pick up point?"

Toms pointed to the chart on his desk. "A Luftwaffe outlying field south of Rohrbeck.

Dicky leaned over the chart. "Any photographs?"

"We should have current pics this afternoon. They're sending in a recce mission this morning."

The two men studied the map.

Toms stood up. "I'm having them send a Hudson out. I think we have to be ready with either aircraft. If the Germans are still in control, we go in the Junkers. Otherwise we take the Hudson."

"Daytime pickup, right?"

"Don't see any choice unless we can coordinate another set up like Seelow. If Jack can illuminate the landing area, we could make it a night go."

"Can we get a message back to Jack?"

Toms turned from the window which overlooked the deserted Dortmund aerodrome. "I don't know. We can get the message to Corry Woods. After that it's up to them."

"I'll draft a message for Jack and Phil Hatcher. We might need some support from Corry Woods on this one."

"Right," Toms said.

The group moved carefully down Bismarkstrasse toward the Brandenburg Gate. Sound of automatic weapons fire came from their right mixed with the occasional report of a tank cannon.

Jack knelt down behind a stone traffic barrier. Karl went down on one knee next to his friend and surveyed the scene.

"Up there on the right. There's a T-34 just around the corner of the building."

He's right, Jack thought, just making out the distinctive square front of the Soviet's main battle tank. Was the tank still in the battle or had it become a victim of the German's Panzerfaust, the only anti-tank weapon left to the skeleton forces defending the Reichschancellery.

"If that tank is operational, it's going to be tough going this way."

"What about the doctor?" Karl asked.

Jack had been avoiding the issue. Any witness to Bormann's escape would compromise their attempt to make the minister "disappear."

"We'll take care of him before we leave for Rohrbeck."

To their front the T-34 now surged ahead from behind the shelter of the cross street.

"The infantry won't be far behind," Karl said with resignation.

The tank slewed left as its tracks threw up dust from the debris in the street. A second T-34 moved onto the street, turning right then stopping for a moment before its main gun fired up Bismarckstrasse. The sound of the fire reverberated from the buildings on either side followed by the roar of the first tank's engine as it moved toward their group. Behind the tank a dozen infantry fanned out on either side of the wide avenue.

"Shit."

The dark shape of the tank grew larger, now less than 100 yards away.

Behind Jack, Stumpfegger stood up, his eyes on the Russians as he stepped backward.

"Get down," Willy yelled at the doctor.

"We've got to get back," Stumpfegger yelled, the terror wild in his voice.

Bormann was now on his feet, his hands on Stumpfegger's arm. He yelled at Jack, "He's right, we must go back."

"Get down, both of you," Jack yelled over the roar of the tank's engine.

The two men stepped backward, their faces toward the Russian tank.

"Stop," Jack yelled. "Stop, NOW!"

Stumpfegger stumbled but Bormann pulled him to his feet. They began to run and stumble down the street both in full panic.

Jack looked at Karl who understood and nodded.

A burst from the MP-40 took both men down, their bodies collapsing in the street.

Jack ran back to where the two men lay motionless. He quickly checked each body then turned toward the advancing tank. "Any ideas?" he yelled at Karl.

"Into that building," Karl called back and the three men ran across the open area and into a wide doorway.

They took cover under the line of windows which faced the street. Broken glass covered the floor around them. Outside the window automatic weapon fire raked the street.

"You killed Bormann," Willy said, his voice incredulous.

Karl was carefully looking out the window. The Soviet infantry had come under fire from an unseen German position. "The Russians are taking fire from somewhere. I think now is the time to make our move."

"What the hell were you doing?" Willy asked again now angry.

Jack grabbed Willy by the arm. "He was following my orders. I'll explain later. For now, drop it."

Willy looked hard at Jack then nodded.

"Let's get the hell out of here," Jack said.

"You don't have to say that more than once," Karl replied. Staying in a crouch, he moved down a wide corridor which ran toward the back of the building.

Jack and Willy followed.

Sergeant Hoffman stood up slowly. The three men advancing across the inner courtyard were the two commandos and the General's son.

Willy climbed the stairs, his eyes anxious when he saw Hoffman.

"All clear?" Karl asked scanning the area down the hallways.

173

"Yes, sir," Hoffman said. "No one has entered the building for over four hours."

"How is my father?"

Hoffman nodded to the door. "The Russian is watching him. He's doing well."

Jack opened the door and immediately saw that General Haselman was sitting in a chair by the table.

The older man looked up from a metal cup of water.

"My son?"

"He's right here, sir."

Willy pushed past Karl and Jack, kneeling down next to his father's chair.

Sergei Volkonsky saw Gregori Malenkov standing next to the large double doorway of a two story brick building which housed the main field communication center for the First Belorussian Corps.

"Pull over there, Sergeant."

Werner Ruess brought the Gaz 4x4 to a stop next to the sandbagged entrance to the building.

Malenkov walked over and slid into the back seat.

"Anything?" Volkonsky asked.

"All reports have been negative. I checked the military police reports and our own internal messages."

Time was running out, he thought. Volkonsky knew that Beria would be demanding a report and he had nothing to tell him. Since their return to the Soviet lines, both Colonels had been implementing a security dragnet for Dmitri Ivanov. Reports on the British team had stopped with no explanation, making them fall back on basic police work to try and find the traitor. The chaos and confusion of the final battle for Berlin hadn't helped their efforts. Trying to get timely reports from across the battle area had proved to be very difficult. Now that the situation was stabilizing they might be able to coordinate the many security teams now swarming over Berlin trying to identify Nazi officials.

Malenkov handed Volkonsky a small map.

"Here are the approximate locations of our security detachments as of this morning."

He looked at the chart which showed the force disposition of the Red Army with the attached NKVD teams which accompanied each division.

"Where are you hiding, Dmitri?"

The four wheel drive Schwimmwagen bounced down the debris littered road. Sergeant Hoffman had proved to be a good driver as he negotiated Berlin streets that looked more like a wasteland than a city. It had taken them almost four hours to make their way west past Spandau. The roads contained a mixture of civilians and military fleeing the Russians. There was a strange quiet across the city. The constant artillery fire of the last two weeks was absent. Surrender of the city was imminent

Covered by a blanket, Dmitri Ivanov now wore the uniform of a Soviet Major. He carried documentation identifying him as Major Denizov the head of an NKVD security team attached to the Eighth Guards Army. General Haselman sat next to Dmitri, wearing the German commando uniform Dmitri had worn until this morning. Willy sat beside his father, an MP-40 on the floorboard next to their feet.

Everyone in the truck kept the weapons concealed as they made their way through the streets. Blending into the surroundings was their best chance with the sun now rising in the eastern sky. The

Germans they passed appeared to be resigned to their fate. Clearly tired and dirty, few of the troops carried weapons. The victors were about to reap the spoils of war and the Germans could do nothing to stop them.

Jack sat in the front seat next to Karl. They both knew they must make it to Rohrbeck within the next twenty four hours for their plan to work. The last message from London gave them a pickup window and the requirement to broadcast the tactical situation in the landing zone. What would they find, Jack wondered? He hoped the landing strip would be abandoned and they could get the aircraft in and out quietly. The urgency of getting to Rohrbeck became stronger as the minutes clicked by.

"Slow down, Sergeant," Karl said. "Stop by those men."

Next to the road, several soldiers wearing the lighting patches of the SS walked in single file.

"Sergeant," Karl yelled at the first man in the line.

Looking over, the Sergeant saw Karl's uniform and straightened up automatically. He walked to the truck.

"Yes, sir," the man said. His eyes told a story of total exhaustion.

"What's happening up ahead?"

"We were told the city was surrendering at noon. Our officer told us to pull back from our positions. The Russians were going to push into the city. That's all I know, sir."

"How far are the Russians?"

The man looked west as if he could see where the Red Army was now. "Maybe 5 or 6 kilometers."

"Any activity up ahead?"

"No, sir. What's left over from a Panzergrenadier battalion, but that's about it."

"Thank you, Sergeant. Good luck."

Hoffman put the truck back in gear and they continued toward Hessestrasse and Rohrbeck.

The Sergeant offered. "If we can get across the river, I know a little used road that runs just south of the airfield."

Jack asked Karl, "Your city, what do you think?"

"I think that's our best chance. If we see too much in our way, we find some place to hide until the situation changes."

Ahead the bridge spanning the river Spree appeared to be intact although there were several burned-out vehicles on the span. At the east end, a defensive position was still manned by troops wearing the Wehrmacht gray.

As they neared the bridge a soldier walked into the roadway holding up his hand.

"Halt!"

"What should I do?" Sergeant Hoffman asked quietly.

Karl could see two MP-34 machine guns manned by the other soldiers.

"Stop, but be ready to drive."

The Corporal looked like a veteran. In his twenties, he needed a shave badly and his uniform was dirty.

"You're driving right into the Russian lines," the man said as he approached Karl's side of the truck. "Sir," he added when he noticed Karl's rank insignia.

"How far ahead, Corporal?" Karl asked, his voice sounding as if he was not really interested.

"Two kilometers, more or less. We expect them here within the hour."

"What are your orders?" Karl continued.

"We haven't had any orders, sir. Our officer was killed two days ago. We remained in our position."

"Corporal, take your men and fall back toward Spaudau. The city will surrender at noon. Until then, make sure your men survive."

The young man looked back with a mixture of surprise and puzzlement. He had probably heard a constant mantra of 'no retreat' Karl thought. Now there was no reason not to retreat and search for the safety of numbers.

"Yes, sir." He saluted.

"Sergeant, let's go," Karl said.

The truck's gears ground as Hoffman put it in 1st and moved forward across the Freybrücke Bridge.

Chapter Twenty-Two

Captain Viktor Mahrkovich threw his used shaving water out the open back door. Using his first chance to clean up in a week, he felt better already. The last two weeks had been as difficult as any since Stalingrad. Heavy fighting as they moved north toward the capital had killed many Germans. His division, the 35th Guards Rifle Division had also lost its share of men. But the end was in sight. Today General Chuikov would take the surrender of Berlin. Finally the enemy would be vanquished.

Originally a regimental political officer, three months ago Mahrkovich had been assigned as an NKVD security officer. The search for Nazi criminals was intensifying and his job was to screen captured German military personnel. Tomorrow they would begin to process prisoners coming out of the city. A temporary holding facility would be constructed on the former Luftwaffe field.

In the distance he saw a column of large trucks on the perimeter road. Those might be the construction troops, he thought.

"Sergeant, take the truck over and see who those men are."

His senior sergeant, Sasha Andreyev looked up from a ration can and nodded.

"Any orders, sir?"

"If they are here to build the compound, have them billet over here by us."

Mahrkovich had already met with the infantry battalion commander whose troops would provide security. He expected they would arrive this afternoon and set up a perimeter while the compound was constructed. Pouring a cup of tea, he walked to the window which overlooked the landing field. Tomorrow, he thought, that field will be covered by German prisoners. Who knows, there might even be a big fish among them. And I will find him out.

Sergeant Andreyev sat down across from Captain Mahrkovich who was reading messages.

"You were right, it's the construction crew."

"Any problems?"

Andreyev shook his head. "They'll be ready to start laying wire as soon as the second part of their convoy gets here. For now they will stake out the ground plan. Their officer wanted to know if you had any special orders?"

Glancing over the priority message from 8th Guards Army headquarters Mahrkovich said, "I'll talk to him." He returned to the message which included a poster of an officer who was wanted by NKVD for questioning. The major in question was to be detained and held for the arrival of a special detachment. Glad I'm not that poor son of a bitch, Mahrkovich thought.

"Let's go," he said, standing up and buckling on his pistol.

The small house was located in the middle of a grove of trees. When the team pulled into the yard, only a single chicken greeted them. Whoever owned the house had obviously departed in a hurry, leaving windows open, clothes and belongings strewn throughout the house and the remains of a small fire still smoldering.

Jack stood at the back window inspecting the landing field a mile in the distance.

"I see vehicles across the field. My guess is Russian," Jack said handing the binoculars to Dmitri.

"No question, those are GAZ and Chevrolet trucks. But it makes me wonder what they're doing here."

Karl asked, "We need to get a message to London. Do we tell them the Russians are holding the area?"

"I can go check to be sure," Dmitri offered.

"Good idea," Karl said.

"I'll walk across the field. I don't think driving up in a German truck is a good idea."

"All right," Jack agreed. "Once you confirm what's going on, we'll send the message. Karl, check out the field. We want to tell them as much as we can about the landing area."

They could see several wrecked aircraft on the southern end of the large field. Other than those obstacles, the field appeared useable.

"Would the Luftwaffe have done anything to sabotage the area before they left," Willy asked.

Karl turned to the General.

"Sir, were you aware of any instructions?"

Despite the long trip, Albert Haselman looked rested and alert. He nodded. "There were standing orders to plant mines in all areas where the enemy might try to land aircraft. But the reality was a total lack of material to carry out those orders. I highly doubt they would have had time, men or ordnance to mine this area."

"Dmitri, try to find out if the Russians know anything."

"I'll be back as soon as I can," Dmitri said, pushing open the door into a backyard.

"I'll keep an eye on him," Jack said, picking up the binoculars and trailing the Russian out the door.

Captain Mahrkovich listened with little enthusiasm as the Engineer Lieutenant explained how they would anchor the barbed wire support stakes to cordon off different sections of prisoners. He noticed a man walking toward them from across the field. That's odd, the thought, I wonder what unit he's from. While the Lieutenant continued to drone on about the technical details of the construction plan, Mahrkovich watched the man approach. He stopped listening to the Lieutenant when he realized the approaching man was a Major.

Turning, the young officers saluted.

"Good morning, Comrade Major," Mahrkovich said.

Returning the salute, Dmitri looked across the wide field surveying the terrain.

"Captain, I'm Major Denizov, Security Section Six. We are tracking a senior Nazi minister we believe is trying to break through our lines in this area. Have you seen any civilian vehicles pass this way in the last two hours?"

He carries himself like a senior NKVD officer, Mahrkovich thought, totally assured.

The young Lieutenant knew to keep his mouth shut.

"No, sir. Only my men and this engineer detachment."

Dmitri looked at the Lieutenant, much like a man looks at a pet dog. "What's going on here," he asked.

"Construction of a holding facility for German prisoners, sir," the young Captain replied stiffly.

Mahrkovich thought the Major looked familiar and wondered why his name didn't sound familiar. I thought I knew all of the senior NKVD officers on the staff, he told himself.

"When will the construction commence," Dmitri asked, his voice still showing little interest.

"Later this morning, Comrade Major," the Lieutenant volunteered.

"Very well. Captain, keep your eyes open for any civilians heading west. You have your screening information I assume?" Dmitri knew the security service transmitted bulletins daily to all detachments which contained persons of interest to be on the lookout for.

"Yes, sir."

As Dmitri turned away, he noticed a look in the Captain's eyes.

Watching Dmitri across the field, Jack wondered how quickly Dicky and Terry Toms could react to the message. He assumed they were still located in Dortmund and would be standing by to execute whatever was needed. Dawn or dusk would be the only reasonable time to request for the landing. The presence of Russian troops would preclude setting up any type of lighting. What the aviators would do about their German transport he didn't know.

His thoughts left possible contingencies as he saw Dmitri raise his hands above his head, the two other men were holding their weapons level at the Russian's chest.

Chapter Twenty-Three

Number 8 Ruston Road
London
May 2, 1945

Phil Hatcher pushed the door open, glancing briefly at the sign over the door, "The Bolyston House." Inside his eyes adjusted to the dim lighting. Most of the tables were empty, not unusual for a pub late morning, even one this close to the docks. He stepped back to the bar and sat down on the end stool.

The bartender wiped his hands on his apron and stepped over to Phil.

"Can I get you something?" His tone neither hostile or friendly.

"I'm looking for Bill O'Hanlon," Phil said quietly.

The man stared back at him.

"Never heard of him."

The man picked up a towel from the bar and began to walk away.

"Tell O'Hanlon that Phil Hatcher wants to talk to him."

Turning, the bartender glared at Phil. "And what makes you think he's here?"

"We can do this easy, or we can do it hard. You decide, because I'm running out of time and patience. You read me?"

The man looked at Phil, trying to decide if he was serious. "Just a minute," he said and walked into the back hallway.

Two minutes later the bartender returned, followed by a large man wearing a tweed overcoat. The grim expression on the man's face changed when he saw Phil.

"By God it is you."

"Liam Hennessy. It's been a long time."

"We heard you left the force," the man said as he leaned on the bar.

"On loan to the army, actually."

"Come on," he said lifting the bar panel up for Phil to walk through.

"He's in back," Liam said.

Bill O'Hanlon, while Irish by birth, ran most of the illegal activities on the London docks. One stint in the Royal Navy had convinced Bill that there were better ways to make a living, particularly if you liked to live high on the vine.

He smiled as Phil entered a very large room that served as O'Hanlon's office and lounge.

"Phil Hatcher, bless my soul!" He rose and offered his hand.

"Bill, you look like the war is being good to you."

O'Hanlon motioned to a seat.

"No complaints. But I'll tell you, that bastard Hitler damned near put me out of business during the blitz. The only thing that kept me going was bringing booze into the city."

"All taxed and legal, I'm sure."

"Of course, bucko. You know me," O'Hanlon said, grinning at Phil. "Can I buy you a drink?"

Phil smiled wryly. "The good stuff?"

"For you? Of course."

Liam brought over a small tray with two glasses and a cut glass container.

O'Hanlon poured the twenty five year old scotch into the glasses.

"So what brings you down here? You back on the job?"

Phil shook his head.

"No, still with the military."

The two men drank.

"Well at least this thing will be over soon." Bill sounded relieved.

Phil considered the Irishman. The two, while on opposite sides of the law, had always maintained a friendly adversarial relationship. Even though he regularly violated many of the laws of the land, O'Hanlon also operated under a code that almost made him a respectable scoundrel. Some day he might be caught, Phil thought, but deep down he knew better. O'Hanlon was ones of the smartest criminals in England.

"Bill, I need your help."

"I didn't think this was a social call." He filled up Phil's glass.

Jack Stewart pushed open the back door of the cottage and saw Karl setting up the radio transmitter.

"The Russians have Dmitri."

Looking up from the small radio, Karl look of surprise was very out of character.

"What did you say?"

Laying his MP-40 on the table, Jack sat down on the single wooden chair in the kitchen.

"I watched him cross the field and talk with two Russians. As he was leaving, they raised their guns and took him prisoner."

"Christ."

"What's happening at the field?"

Jack shook his head. "Looks like a platoon around that building. I didn't see any prepared defenses or heavy weapons."

General Haselman had been watching their exchange. "What will you do?"

Karl looked at Jack and said, "Try to get him back."

"We can help," Willy said, indicating himself and Sergeant Hoffman.

Jack looked at his watch. "If we have any chance at all, it has to be fast. I can only think of one way and it's a long shot."

Karl snorted, "We specialize in long shots."

General Haselman smiled.

Two motorcycle police led the GAZ 4 x 4 truck around a damaged portion of the main autobahn enroute to the Rohrbeck prisoner holding facility. It had been a slow trip since leaving sector headquarters. Most of the roads were torn up or clogged with people. They had passed civilian refugees walking west from Berlin, probably not realizing the

Red Army surrounded the entire city. For those displaced people, life was going to become very difficult.

But Sergei Volkonsky did not notice, nor did he care about the wreckage left after the battle for Berlin. All that occupied his mind now was to get to Rohrbeck and confirm the NKVD detachment had Dmitri Ivanov in custody. His frustration at losing Ivanov's trail had built as the battle for the capitol came to a close. He knew the only hope they might still capture the traitor would be a lucky encounter.

The message from Captain Mahrkovich had been the answer to his problem, if this prisoner really was Ivanov. According to Mahrkovich, he fit the description and spoke with a Georgian accent. It must be him, he thought and I will make him tell me everything he knows. Then I will kill him.

"How long will it take to get to this place?" Gregori Malenkov asked.

"With the condition of the roads, it could be several hours," Sergeant Reuss replied.

"We should get there before dark?"

"Yes, sir," the Sergeant said, turning hard to miss a deep bomb crater.

Karl switched the radio to standby then turned the power switch off.

Jack looked at his friend.

Both men knew they had set events in motion that might destroy both of them and everything they had worked for over the last two years.

Karl walked across the small room and sat down looking out the window into the garden.

"Quite a gamble, Colonel."

Turning, Karl saw General Haselman smiling at him.

"Herr General, we're willing to risk everything to get our man back."

"The Russians are your allies. You're risking much more than just men's lives."

Karl rubbed his eyes, the strain of two weeks beginning to wear him down.

"Sir, we both saw what the Russians did as they moved west. I've also seen how the British do things over the last two years. Those two systems will never co exist. They might have tolerated each other to defeat Hitler, but never will they get along."

Albert Haselman remembered the British officers he had met after the war and the Americans in Berlin. Dietrich is right, he thought. There is hope for the future, as bleak as it seems now.

"Colonel, I don't disagree."

Chapter Twenty-Four

Luftwaffe Auxillary Field 23
Rohrbeck, Germany
May 2, 1945

Dmitri Ivanov sat on a straight-backed wooden chair, his hands tied behind his back. Captain Mahrkovich had searched all of his pockets, removing the fake identity papers which sat on the table.

"Shouldn't those big shots be here by now?" Sergeant Andreyev asked.

"Anytime, I'm sure."

The Captain had been told that Colonels Volkonsky and Malenkov we enroute to take the prisoner into custody. Mahrkovich had heard of Volkonsky. It was rumored the man worked directly for Beria. That thought bothered the young officer. Anything connected with the Commissar for State Security could be very dangerous for anyone involved.

"I've got most of the men helping the engineers unload their trucks. That Lieutenant asked if we could help them string wire tomorrow and I said yes."

Captain Mahrkovich nodded. "Until we get the camp set up, we won't be doing any screening. We might as well lend them a hand." He stood and walked to the single window. "And you, Major Ivanov, your screening will take place far from here."

Dmitri saw the look on the man's face, both of them knowing he was referring to Moscow. But why take me there, Dmitri wondered. They can do anything they need to right here. He ignored the Captain.

Andreyev began to light the candles which were located in lanterns around the room. Soon the room was lit by flickering candle light.

The sound of an engine came from outside and the door opened. The sentry saluted and said, "A car is here, Comrade Captain."

The young soldier moved out of the door as Sergei Volkonsky pushed past him.

Mahrkovich stood to attention, facing the large man who had his eyes fixed on the prisoner.

"Sir, I…"

"Get out of here," Volkonsky barked without looking at the Captain.

"Yes, sir."

Gregori Malenkov entered as Mahrkovich and his sergeant made a fast exit.

"Dmitri, it is you." Malenkov smiled broadly. "You led us on quite a chase."

Ivanov didn't reply, he could only focus on Volkonsky's gray eyes and the hate he saw within them.

The tall colonel walked over and sat down at the table.

Malenkov moved behind Dmitri and pulled a knife from the sheath on his belt. He looked at Volkonsky who nodded.

Reaching down, Malenkov cut the ropes binding Dmitri's hands behind his back.

Dmitri began to massage his wrists then his shoulders.

"Tell me why I shouldn't shoot you right now?" Volkonsky asked.

"Perhaps you should," Dmitri said quietly. "But I suspect your orders are to return me to Moscow."

"Before I do that, I want to know what happened."

Dmitri knew that he was probably already under a sentence of death. Why should I tell them anything, he thought?

"You might actually survive this, if and I say, if you have some reason that could possible explain your actions."

"And what does Moscow think I've done?"

"My, our little traitor has quite the spirit," Malenkov added. "Two days at Lubyanka will cure you of that," he said, the humor now gone from his voice.

Ignoring his comrade, Volkonsky laughed. "What have you done? Joining the British Secret Service. Conducting a covert mission with the British and killing six Soviet soldiers in Berlin. To say nothing of compromising state security by failing in your mission to Falkenberg."

Dmitri looked at the man who used to be his best friend. He remembered the times together, the danger and the friendship. Now that had all disappeared in the brutal reality of the moment.

"When I regained consciousness two weeks after Falkenberg, I was already in England. I knew we had failed and that was enough for Beria to have me shot. I also knew that I would never be trusted again after my time with the British."

The two Soviet Colonels listened, their expressions giving no hint of their thoughts.

"There is a huge difference from requesting asylum to actually participating in a field mission for the other side," Volkonsky said, his voice now more controlled.

"Lying in that hospital gave me time to think. I had always been loyal to the party and the communist cause. But what I saw as the Red Army moved west was something I did not agree with."

"You son of a bitch," Malenkov blurted out.

"I saw our own people in the Ukraine killed to make sure the party would remain dominant after the Germans were beaten."

"Do you expect me to believe you never knew what we had been doing for years to ensure party dominance?" Volkonsky asked, sounding incredulous.

"I had convinced myself otherwise and looked the other way. But now I found I couldn't do that anymore."

Volkonsky shook his head. "You are a fool."

"And so will you take me back to that bastard Beria?"

Sergei Volkonsky knew that once back in Moscow, the interrogators in Lubyanka would make his last days a living nightmare. Did Dmitri's previous service to the state earn him a quicker and more painless end? What would Beria do to them if they didn't bring Ivanov back to Moscow?

"Do they have anything decent to drink around this shit hole?" Volkonsky asked aloud as he walked to the door.

"Are you sure about this?" Willy asked his father.

"Very sure," the General said, easing himself behind the wheel of the schwimmwagen.

Willy nodded and squeezed his father's arm. "Here," he said, handing his pistol to the General.

"No, you might need it."

Holding up the MP-40, Willy smiled. "I can handle this with my good arm."

Dieter Hoffman appeared from behind the truck, a fuel can in his hand.

"Sir, I was able to siphon about two liters. Will that be enough?"

"That will be fine, Sergeant," the General replied. "Take it to Commander Stewart."

Karl and Jack continued to stack broken furniture and paper in the cottage's parlor. Small kindling from the woodpile behind the house also was stacked in and around the rest of the debris.

"Sir, here is the fuel. There are still five or six liters left in the tank if we need it."

"Set it down by the window, Sergeant," Jack said.

Karl stood up from pushing two logs under the small wood table. "I think we need to pull down those curtains and break all the windows."

Jack looked around and agreed, "More air, more fire. Sergeant, would you make sure all the windows are broken? Start here and then do the entire cottage."

"Yes, sir."

Karl walked across the room and stood next to Jack.

"About an hour?"

Jack nodded. Events had taken over and they were rushing to an end none of them would, have ever dreamed of.

194

Chapter Twenty-Five

Forty Miles east of Rohrbeck
8,000 Feet
May 2, 1945

It was quiet in the darkened cabin of the Hudson transport. Capable of carrying 12 fully equipped soldiers, only seven men occupied the canvas seats. Dressed in the olive drab uniforms of United States paratroopers, the men sat without talking, their distinctive helmets on the empty seats next to Thompson sub-machine guns. In addition to the shoulder flash of the 101st Airborne Division, each man wore a U.S. flag armband.

Captain Terry Howe looked across the aisle at Gerhard Lutjens, who was staring into the night. Two men from different countries, different backgrounds, now comrades who trusted each other with their lives.

"Not exactly how you planned to return to Berlin?"

Gerhard laughed. "Certainly not dressed as an American Sergeant."

The two men had been on two missions together behind German lines. They accepted the dangers of combat behind the lines, but this was not something either of them ever envisioned. Terry had wondered why Jack had him procure the uniforms and equipment they were using tonight. Jack must have been a Boy Scout, Terry thought, always prepared.

"Just try not to say too much. As good as your English is, your accent is definitely German."

"I think we both need to keep our mouths shut and let the Colonel run the show," Terry replied.

Sitting in the first row behind the cockpit a large man sat by himself, his eyes closed, totally relaxed. The single silver star on his collar identified him as a Brigadier General. The crossed rifles signified infantry. But what his uniform did not display was his qualification as an Army Ranger.

Colonel Jim Ronhaar had originally trained with the British Commandos in 1942. A veteran of Dieppe, North Africa and Normandy, he led an elite American unit that operated for the OSS. The four men with him were the best combat operatives in the European Theater. Trained in every aspect of covert operations, they had an impressive record on the continent. Since the invasion, they had conducted six critical missions behind the German lines. Now they were going behind Soviet lines. A call from Winston Churchill to Dwight Eisenhower was required to put Ronhaar's team on the mission.

Terry Howe got up and walked forward in the darkened cabin. He swayed slightly as the aircraft reacted to the turbulent air. "How long," he said over the noise of the engines.

Dicky Thompson looked over his left shoulder.

"We'll be in the area in twelve minutes. Then we have to spot the signal and the landing area."

196

Terry looked forward out the cockpit window, seeing scattered clouds scudding across the night sky.

"I'll get them ready."

Colonel Ronhaar's arms were crossed on his chest, his expression one of total calm.

"Colonel?"

Jim Ronhaar's eyes opened. He sat up, uncrossing his arms.

"What's up, Captain?"

"We're ten minutes from the area, Colonel."

"Right. Let my men know."

Terry nodded and moved back to the sleeping men.

"These winds have been a bitch, tonight," Terry Toms said, adjusting the compass. "But judging by the water patterns, that's Potsdam and Rohrbeck is at our 11:00 o'clock, five miles. I'd say we're in the area."

Dicky checked his watch.

"Pretty close to the time," he noted.

"Now let's see how lucky Stewart is. Taking her down."

Sergei Volkonsky grimaced as he swallowed the last brandy from the chipped ceramic mug.

"If I take you back to Moscow, you're a dead man." His voice slightly slurred.

Dmitri held his metal mess cup, staring into the dark liquid.

"So let me walk out of here."

"Then I'm a dead man," he laughed, filling his mug from the half-empty bottle on the table.

"Then come with me," Dmitri said, his words slurred as well. "Tell that bastard Beria to fuck off."

197

Volkonsky stared at his former friend.

"You're as stupid as most Georgians. You don't walk away from Beria. No matter where you go, they'll find you. Look at Trotsky." He took a deep drink. "Besides, Malenkov would happily put a bullet in both of us."

Dmitri looked at Volkonsky with surprise.

"I stole his wife and he never did like you," he snorted as he finished his brandy.

Gregori Malenkov lay on a sleeping roll next to the fire, a towel covering his eyes.

Flames leaped up the walls of the cottage as the debris and fuel caught fire. Standing in the front yard, Jack and Karl knew the die was cast. As the flames curled out of the broken windows and caught on the edge of the roof, they both climbed into the truck.

General Albert Haselman shoved the transmission into the lowest gear and engaged the clutch.

"Same location, correct?"

"Yes, Herr General, the same place. Winds are still out of the east and I think that's our safest approach for the aircraft."

Five minutes later the General brought the truck to a stop on the edge of the landing field. Both headlights had been cleaned of the black paint that allowed only a thin ribbon of light to escape. The area for several hundred feet was brightly illuminated. In the distance the flames from the cottage were clearly visible in the dark night sky.

"We've done all we can do. Now it's up to Dicky," Jack said.

"There it is," Terry Toms exclaimed, pointing at the bright fire on the ground right on their nose.

"Tallyho," Dicky responded. "Look there, 11 o'clock from the fire.

"I see it. Gear down, flaps down."

"Gear coming down," Dicky said, watching the transition lights illuminate. Under them they could hear the main landing gear swinging out into the wind stream.

"Standby for landing," Dicky yelled to the cabin and turned on the landing lights of the Hudson.

The tops of trees were immediately visible and Toms added power to stop his rate of descent.

The lights from the truck on the ground were now a quarter of a mile on the nose.

"Here we go," Toms said, pulling the power back and setting the landing attitude.

For five long seconds the small transport maintained its descent and then the wheels hit the ground with loud thumps.

"Let's go," Karl yelled and the schwimmwagen accelerated after the aircraft, which was now rolling out across the field.

"They're heading for the control building," Jack called out as the truck raced after the aircraft. The men started coughing as dust from the Hudson and gasoline fumes engulfed them. In the headlights it appeared there were two vehicles parked at the building and a group of tents just to the west.

"Head to this side of the building," Karl directed and the General turned the speeding truck to the right, the structure now only 200 yards ahead.

As the Hudson jerked to a stop, Dicky yelled, "Out! Out!"

The rear access hatch popped open and men began to emerge, fanning out as they walked toward the building.

Several Soviets soldiers stood next to a fire near their tent area. From the far side of the encampment two armed sentries appeared and walked toward Colonel Ronhaar, who approached with one of his men.

"This is General Anderson, U.S. Army," the man called out in Russian. "Who is in charge here?"

Captain Mahrkovich had heard the aircraft and now emerged from one of the tents where he had been exiled after the arrival of Volkonsky.

"I am Captain Mahrkovich."

"General Anderson is here to meet with General Chuikov," the Ranger translator said.

Mahrkovich approached and saluted.

"I'm afraid I don't know where the General is at this time."

Ronhaar turned to his man and said, "Tell them we were told he would be in Potsdam in the morning to meet with me. We need to discuss our travel arrangements."

Sergeant Andreyev walked up tentatively as the rest of the Soviet soldiers returned to their fire.

"Certainly, sir."

Terry Howe pushed the door of the control building open and stepped inside followed by Gerhard and one of the Rangers. All of them held Thompsons level at their waists.

Sergei Volkonsky sat up with a start, lifting his head from the table. He began to speak but was interrupted by the Ranger who said harshly in Russian, "Don't move."

On the ground, Gregori Malenkov sat up, obviously confused, having been awakened from a deep sleep.

"What the fuck is going on?" Volkonsky demanded angrily.

Terry ignored the big man and walked over to Dmitri, who looked up sleepily but said nothing. Motioning with his weapon, Terry directed Dmitri toward the door.

Volkonsky began to stand up.

"What are you doing," he said, the anger now rising in his voice.

"Getting ready to kill you if you don't sit down," the Ranger said.

The Colonel sat down, his eyes bright in the candlelight.

Terry escorted Dmitri out the door.

"You're Americans," Malenkov exclaimed.

The soldier said nothing, but kept the Thompson leveled at the two men.

Gerhard proceeded to gag and tie both men like pigs going to market.

It's lights now off, the truck slid to a stop beside the control building. Karl jumped from the rear seat as Jack opened the door and headed for the front of the building.

Willy Haselman jumped out the left side of the truck and ran to the corner of the building. He surveyed the scene and then motioned to Dieter Hoffman.

The Sergeant opened the General's door and said, "Sir, it is time."

Albert Haselman looked at his orderly with surprise. "What does that mean?"

"We have orders to get you on the aircraft, Herr General."

The older man looked at the Sergeant, then smiled.

"I think this is as far as I go, my friend."

Willy ran over.

"Father, let's go."

"You take the Sergeant, I'll make sure things are taken care of here."

"You're going. Those are Stewart's orders to me and he speaks for Churchill. Your duty is to escape the Russians so we can help rebuild this country. Now let's go, or we'll carry you."

Major General Albert Haselman, Chief of Staff, Army Group Vistula, smiled back at his son and old friend.

"As you wish, gentlemen. I am too tired to fight both of you," he said, then laughed.

Moving quickly, Karl checked out the area, noting a group of men talking over by the tents. The wooden stairs on the front of the control building ran up to a single door, which was closed. He turned to see Jack next to him.

"Well?" the German asked.

"Let's go," Jack said and they started up the stairs.

The door opened and both men knelt down, their MP-40's aimed at the two men exiting the door.

"Wait," Jack said quickly, "They're ours."

Coming down the stairs they saw Dmitri followed by Terry.

"Are you all right?" Jack asked Dmitri.

"Happy to be alive," he responded.

"There are some really angry Russians up there," Terry said, turning his head toward the control building.

Karl started to move up the stairs.

"Gerhard has things under control," Terry said.

"No doubt," Karl said, taking the steps two at a time.

As his interpreter haggled back and forth with the Soviet officer about the travel arrangements, Colonel Ronhaar watched the Hudson idling in the darkness. He noted his two men at the edge of the building, almost hidden in the shadows. His interpreter kept up a steady barrage of what Ronhaar assumed were questions as the two Russians took notes and nodded. Occasionally the officer would interrupt the young American and a heated discussion would take place. Ronhaar had directed the Sergeant to nit-pick every detail of their supposed transportation requirements and then launch into a demand for quarters, food, aviation gasoline and vodka. He saw figures moving from the building back to the aircraft and could only hope the lack of firing meant that Captain Howe had surprised the Russians inside.

Ronhaar saw three quick flashes from a light in the cockpit and knew it was time.

"Tell the Russian I am confident we can work everything out. We will go back to the aircraft to get our gear and tell the pilots to shut down the engines. Tell them our first priority is to get some aviation fuel here by morning to refuel our aircraft."

He waited while the Sergeant conveyed his message. The Russians nodded.

"Have we got everyone?" Jack asked Terry Howe who stood in the aisle behind Jack.

"I've counted twice. Everyone's here."

Jack turned back to Wing Commander Toms.

"Let's get out of here."

203

Captain Viktor Mahrkovich stood in the darkness wondering where in the hell he would get aviation gasoline for this American General? As he went over options in his mind he noticed the American aircraft was turning south and its engines were revving up. The aircraft began to accelerate for takeoff and Mahrkovich knew something was very wrong.

"Come on," he yelled at Sergeant Andreyev and began to run toward the control building.

Chapter Twenty-Six

East London
2 May, 1945

In her younger years, Alice Hollingsworth had gained a small level of notoriety among the London dance hall crowd. A pretty face and tolerable voice had entertained a generation of dock workers and teamsters in East London. However a love of the good life and two failed marriages had taken their toll on Alice. Now she ran a modest apartment house for a landlord who she seldom ever saw and drank herself to sleep most nights of the week.

"Where is that worthless bag of bones," she said to herself opening the first floor storage room in search of Mr. Harris, the building's elderly maintenance man.

Her search unsuccessful, she walked down the hall toward the stairs which led to the second floor. Maybe the old bastard's up there, she told herself.

As she started up the stairs, she glanced up to see Mr. Walker coming down. Smiling brightly, she subconsciously thrust her chest out, her ample breasts still able to get men to look.

"Well good morning, Mr. Walker," she said in her cheeriest voice.

"Uh, hello, Mrs. Hollingsworth. Good day to you."

She watched his eyes stray to her chest, feeling a small victory in a day that otherwise had been totally shitty.

"You're out and about early today," she offered as they stopped on the stairs. While she wanted to prolong their encounter, it was clear Mr. Walker would rather be on his way.

"Meeting a friend for tea," he said noncommittally.

She eyed him for a long moment.

"Is everything alright with your room?" she asked.

"Quite alright, thank you for asking. Now I really must go if I don't want to be late."

"Of course, please don't let me hold you up."

She stared at the man as he walked down the stairs. He's obviously a man of refined breeding, she thought to herself. But I don't understand why he dyes his hair that horrid black. And the white area on his upper lip had certainly been covered by facial hair until just recently. If I didn't know better, she said to herself, then her eyes opened wide.

"Bloody hell!"

Twenty minutes east of Rohrbeck, Wing Commander Toms began a slow climb, knowing they were well east of any Soviet night fighter patrol areas.

"Jack?"

Stewart turned to see Gerhard Lutjens behind him in the aisle.

"Terry and I have to talk to you before we land."

206

Jack saw Terry in the last row of seats looking at them. He could tell by Gerhard's tone that it was not good news.

Phil Hatcher stood in the circle of light cast by a single overhead light outside the hangar. He watched the two engines on the Hudson wind down. The ground crew had already chocked the main wheels and waited for the rear access hatch to open. He knew that Karl Dietrich would take the news of Eva's death with little outside emotion. But Karl was also very passionate about the important things in his life. Phil had watched the relationship rebuild between Karl and Eva for over two years. There was no doubt they loved each other and he had assumed they would marry after the war. Now that was all over.

In the distance he saw Jack and Karl coming in from the Hudson. He walked out slowly to meet them.

"Welcome back," Phil said, offering his hand to both men. "Do you want to send a message to the Brigadier?"

Jack looked grim, while Karl remained impassive.

"They're fueling the plane now. Dicky said he can have us back in England by daybreak, but we still need to let Greene know what happened."

The three men walked toward the hangar.

"Understood," Phil said.

"Send it 'most secret' eyes only Greene. He can decide if he wants to wake up the PM or not. Tell him mission complete, option two exercised. No casualties."

"Right. Anything else?"

"We both need a drink," Jack said.

"What can you tell me?" Karl asked. It was the first time he had spoken since landing.

Phil outlined what they knew of the final week of Eva's life.

Karl said nothing as he listened, his mouth set in a tight line.

Jack asked a question here and there, but let Phil run down events as they had played out, including the night that Eva had died.

"Karl, I'm sorry," Phil finally said, his brief completed. "If I hadn't lost the car, she might still be alive."

"What do we know of Kent?" Karl asked, ignoring Phil's remark.

"He's disappeared. We don't know if the Russians have him hidden away or they might have him out of the country already."

Karl stared down at the table, whether trying to contain his anger or hide his emotion, Jack didn't know.

Phil continued, "If the Russians have him, it's going to be very difficult to intercept him without risking big problems with the Soviet government."

Looking up, both men saw a look in Karl's eyes they had never seen before.

"I don't care," he said quietly, getting up and walking out of the room.

"There's more," Phil said after Karl was gone. "Do we fill him in now or wait."

"Bring me up to speed. We'll let him go at his own speed. But tell Gerhard I want him to stay close to Karl. I don't need him doing something on his own."

"Right."

"Jack, wake up."

Phil Hatcher knelt in the Hudson's aisle and shook Jack's knee.

"Huh?"

"General Haselman is unconscious."

"His Sergeant was trying to wake him up when we hit the Channel and he couldn't."

They found Willy leaning over his father, who lay back, his head to one side.

"What happened?" Jack asked.

"My father told Sergeant Hoffman he was tired. He asked that he be awakened when we neared England."

Jack put him hand on the General's neck, feeling a pulse which was slow and erratic.

"Keep him warm and watch him," Jack said, heading up the aisle to the cockpit.

"The General's unconscious. What's the closest airfield to the Ramsgate Hospital?"

Terry Toms looked over his shoulder and said, "Hendon, I should think. A quick ride to the hospital from there."

"Can we land there?"

"I'll land this crate anywhere you want me to, Commander."

Two hours later the small group stood outside the General's room in Ward D of the military hospital. Doctor Roger Hanson had been called in and Jack had briefed his old friend on what they knew of the General's injury.

After twenty minutes with the General, Roger emerged from the room, his face serious.

"Jack, he's resting now and his vital signs are stable. I want to keep him under observation for now and then run tests this afternoon."

When Willy asked Jack in German for the prognosis, Roger Hanson showed no surprise.

He told the group that it was too early to tell anything definitive.

"You all look like you need food and rest," Roger added. "Give us time to do what we can. I'll let you know as soon as anything happens."

Two sedans picked the team up from the hospital. One left directly for Corry Woods. The other headed southeast toward MI-6's headquarters at Baker Street.

"Ever been to London, Willy?" Jack asked.

Haselman shook his head and smiled slightly.

"Not London, but I did visit Paris. It was 1940."

Jack looked at Willy, then realized the twist.

"Baker Street is only 30 minutes from the hospital," Jack continued. "We'll get you settled there."

"What will happen to me?" Willy asked.

"Let's not worry about that right now. Your assistance to our mission was critical and we will not forget that. This war is ending, everything is in transition. Worry about your father for now. We'll sort out what to do later."

"Thank you," Willy said, turning to stare out the window.

Pamela Thompson opened the door to the Library.

"May I come in?" she asked.

Sitting on the couch and staring out the small window, Karl answered, "Yes, of course."

She sat down on the couch and put her hand on his arm. "Karl, I am so sorry."

He nodded.

Pam had known him for two years and they had become good friends. On the mission to Falkenberg they had developed a respect and affection that was mutual. Now she didn't know how to help her friend deal with his loss.

"Did they tell you she was working for MI-5?" he asked.

Pam nodded, the accusation echoing in the small room. "There had to be a reason," she said. "You and I both know that. She loved you and would never betray that."

"But she did."

Karl had learned everything he could about the chain of events leading to Eva's death. He had come to the same conclusion that Phil had, she had been sending information to the Russians. He had to know why.

Two days later the General's condition remained unchanged. Roger Hanson told Jack there was no way to tell when he might emerge from what now appeared to be a coma.

On their return to Baker Street, Jack received a message that Noel Greene wanted to see him. He told Willy to get ready to leave for Corry Woods and went upstairs to the Brigadier's office.

"I received your message. The Prime Minister wants to see both of us at our earliest convenience as he put it. Your explanation of the events that night was very clear. There was no choice?"

"No, sir. If Bormann had left our immediate area alive he most likely would have been captured by the Russians. I wasn't going to try and subdue him in the middle of a street under machine gun fire. Now, he will never talk. It will also be very difficult to identify the remains. The most acceptable resolution available in my opinion."

"Let's hope Winston feels the same way." He got up from the chair, reaching for his jacket on the coat rack. "Any update on General Haselman?"

"No, sir. He's stable, but still in a coma. Major Haselman and I plan to go to Corry Woods this afternoon."

"Why am I thinking that you are back in the recruiting business again?"

Jack laughed.

"Sir, if it hadn't been for Major Haselman, we would have never connected with Bormann. He was totally under control in a very tough situation. With the war winding down in Europe, we're going to need agents in Germany for the future."

"I agree, just go slow. Now, the PM is waiting."

Chapter Twenty-Seven

East London
May 3, 1945

Jack looked around the large office which was not what he expected in this part of town.

"Some of those paintings on the wall look authentic," he said.

"They probably are, "Phil answered, "O'Hanlon is known as an art lover. For a gangster he's actually a pretty refined bloke."

The men sat on the large couch waiting for the office's owner to arrive. The meeting had been initiated by O'Hanlon with a phone call to Phil at Corry Woods.

The door opened and Jack saw a man in his 40's, medium build, well groomed and wearing a sport coat.

Phil stood up and introduced Jack.

"Bill, this is my boss, Commander Jack Stewart. Jack, meet Bill O'Hanlon."

The two men shook hands and Jack Stewart sensed that O'Hanlon was much more than a dockyard tough.

"Commander?"

"That's right," Jack answered.

"Which Navy?"

"Royal Navy. Why do you ask?"

"That's an American accent if I've ever heard one."

"Also true. But it's a long story and I'm sure you're a busy man."

O'Hanlon laughed and motioned them back to the couch. He walked over to the bar and poured three drinks. Handing each man a drink, he walked back to his desk and sat down.

"To your health, gentlemen."

They all drank.

"Bill, what do you have for us?" Phil asked.

The older man took another drink and sat back.

"A most intriguing story that I heard from a lady I know."

They sat waiting for his story, but he stopped to light a cigarette and exhale.

"This woman runs a small rooming house near the Exeter dock. After your last visit, I sent out the word we were looking for a gent that fit a particular description. God bless Alice, she noticed this man at her place had dyed his hair and shaved his mustache. He fit the height and weight you gave us and he had started living there only recently. My guess is that this Walker is the man you're looking for."

"We very much want to get our hands on him," Jack said.

"Then I'm guessing His Majesty's Government would be willing to pay highly for the information," O'Hanlon said, crushing out his cigarette in the ashtray.

"They might," Phil interrupted. "But I'm thinking you would feel better knowing you had contributed something to the war effort."

"That's what I like about you, Hatcher, balls of brass and not afraid to use them."

"Will you help us," Jack asked.

O'Hanlon grinned. "It would be my great pleasure. Knowing that in the future the authorities would view my assistance in a very positive way."

Hatcher smiled. "We wouldn't have it any other way."

Phillip Kent walked quickly down the alley, his mind racing as he tried to understand what had just happened. Earlier in the day he had again checked the drop location at Marlybone, but nothing had been left for him. His patience with Krishkin running out, he had called the contact number at the embassy to find it was out of service. As the panic set in, Kent had dialed a general access number at the embassy and asked for Mr. Nickolev, a code name he was to use in any emergency. The operator told him that there was no one by the name of Nickolev at the embassy. Now in full panic he asked for Krishkin, but was told his contact was "not available."

What was happening he asked himself? He returned to the docks to think. Was there a mistake at the embassy? Or were they shutting the door on him? That made no sense. Why would they sacrifice someone with the depth of knowledge he possessed of British Intelligence. He had been a loyal agent for over a decade. His contributions to the ultimate victory of the party could not be denied.

He turned onto the main street and walked toward his apartment building, turning his coat collar up and tying to look as unobtrusive as possible.

Konstantin Rostov had always enjoyed London. Perhaps it was the history, maybe the people, but there was electricity here that he had never felt in Moscow. Riding into the city after an all night flight from the Soviet capital, he was looking forward to seeing Noel Greene.

Once checked into the Claridge, Rostov freshened up and waited for the next move. The morning papers from London lay on the table and he sat down to wait.

Twenty minutes later, one of his security officers knocked and informed him the meeting was ready to commence two doors down the hall.

Noel Greene was standing in the center of the room when Rostov entered, both men smiled in recognition.

"You look well, Noel."

"As do you, my friend. Please sit down, there is much to discuss."

Greene turned to a large man standing behind the couch, clearly a security agent.

"Why don't you wait outside, Harrington, we will be fine."

Rostov reciprocated, asking his agent to also retire to the hallway.

After small talk and cups of tea were poured, Noel Greene sat back and crossed his legs.

"Thank you for travelling here at such short notice."

Rostov nodded. "This is important to both of us."

"As you can imagine, we are very unhappy with the turn of events. Kent had risen to the top ranks in MI-5 and was destined for greater responsibilities."

And he would still have reached those if Beria had not interfered, Rostov thought.

"You can understand the British government would like this entire episode to end quietly."

"If I were in your position I would feel the same," Rostov said.

"And at our moment of triumph over the Nazis, neither of our governments need a scandal."

"I would not disagree."

"We originally proposed a quiet exchange and you had indicated you were not adverse to the idea."

Rostov took a sip of his tea and nodded.

"Correct."

"However that was when we believed you would get Kent out of the country before we could apprehend him."

"And something has changed?"

"We have located Kent. Our intention is to eliminate him with no publicity."

The surprise on Rostov's face made Green smile.

"Out of character for us?"

"Very much so."

"But we know that by doing so, we risk starting a chain reaction between our respective services which we don't desire and hope you feel the same way."

Konstantin Rostov looked at Greene, surprised at his friend's candor.

"Are you asking for our permission to move forward with this?"

"Actually, yes." Greene said.

"You will interrogate Kent, then kill him and ask us not to take any reciprocal action?"

Greene's expression was hard. "I will tell you that we won't interrogate him."

Rostov realized what Greene meant. For the Soviets to protect any information that Kent might have, they had to agree to his termination with no retaliation. What Greene didn't know was that Beria had already decided that he would not risk anything to save Kent. This was a bonus.

"Who did he kill?"

"One of my agents, a German girl we turned three years ago."

"I'm sorry."

They sat in silence as Greene poured more tea.

"I agree to you proposal," Rostov finally said. "With one qualification."

"What is that?"

"Tell me why you sent your team into Berlin?"

Greene stood and walked over to the window.

"What do you know of an organization called the network?"

Rostov thought back to the many reports he had read, but the term didn't sound familiar.

Greene continued, "As the war started to go the wrong way, a confederation of German officers, primarily from the intelligence community formed an organization dedicated to overthrowing Hitler. The July plot was one of their efforts."

"We assumed there was more to it than was reported."

"One of the key members was in danger in Berlin and we felt compelled to rescue him."

Evaluating what he was being told, Rostov felt that it had merit, but decided to push for more.

"Why would you risk so much for one man?"

"Konstantin, you know our old-fashioned sense of honor."

The Russian laughed.

"Yes, we will never understand you. Will you tell me who it was?"

"One of the men we feel will help Germany recover from the Nazi scourge. His name is Haselman, General Albert Haselman."

"I've heard of him."

"And I'm sure you understand why we wanted to get Dmitri Ivanov back also."

Greene nodded. "I do, but I can't make him part of this arrangement."

"Understood."

"So everything is settled?"

"Yes. And let us hope we can maintain a level of professional respect in the future."

"Let me start by buying you dinner tonight at my club."

"I would enjoy that very much."

Karl Deitrich walked up the stairs behind Jack Stewart. They saw Phil Hatcher at the top of the second landing.

"Is he still in his room?" Jack asked quietly.

Hatcher nodded.

"Let's go," Jack said, looking down the hall.

The worn wooden door had a small wood block with the number 26 carved in it. The three men looked around one more time as Phil slowly inserted a key into the lock and turned. The door swung open slowly, the interior of the room dark.

Karl pulled a pistol from his jacket pocket and quietly entered. With the Walther in his hand, Jack followed.

Roger Hanson waited at the entrance to Ward D with Gerhard Lutjens. They saw Willy Haselman walking down the corridor toward the security desk.

"Thank you for coming," Roger said. "I'm afraid my German is very rusty."

"I am happy to help, particularly with good news."

Willy, wearing a plain brown suit, looked anxious.

Gerhard offered his hand.

"Herr Major, Doctor Hanson asked me to translate."

"What is the news?" Willy asked, his concern obvious.

"Your father's condition has improved. He's awake and talking. Doctor Hanson wanted you to see him right away. He will answer any questions you have."

Looking at the doctor, Willy asked simply, "Will he live?"

Roger waited for Gerhard's translation.

"For now he's out of danger," Roger said. "With rest and recuperation he should do well. The combination of his wound and total exhaustion simply caught up with him."

Willy wiped his eyes.

"Can I see him?"

Roger smiled. "He's been asking for you and we don't like to keep generals waiting."

Phillip Kent stirred and began to roll over when he felt the barrel of a gun against the side of his face.

"Remain very still or I will kill you as you lie there," a voice said from the darkness, the accent German.

The light came on and Kent's heart went cold as he saw Karl Dietrich holding the gun against his throat.

"Kent, you're under arrest for murder and treason." Phil Hatcher stepped next to Karl who had pulled the sheets down to Kent's waist. He reached down and roughly pulled Kent's arms behind his back and attached a set of handcuffs.

Karl reached down and pulled Kent on his back, pushing the pistol barrel into the man's mouth.

Kent looked up in terror to see a wild look in Karl's eyes.

"I should kill you right here," Karl said, his fury barely contained.

"Karl, no! Not here," Jack said harshly.

Pulling the hammer back on the pistol, Karl only had to apply the slightest pressure and Kent's head would explode on the pillow.

"Jack, we can save the government a trial and ourselves a lot time."

Karl's eyes bore into Kent, the silence in the room overwhelming. He slowly pulled the barrel out of Kent's mouth and stepped back, the gun still pointed and the traitor's chest.

"Get him up," Karl said.

Phil pulled Kent roughly to his feet.

"Pull on his pants and button this jacket around him," Jack said, handing Kent's overcoat to Phil.

Albert Haselman's eyes turned as Willy walked up to the bed. He smiled slightly.

Willy reached down and took his father's hand.

"You had me worried."

"I feel much better," his father said in a quiet but steady voice.

"The doctor said you will be fine with rest."

The General nodded.

Roger approached the bed.

"I think that rest should start now. Major, why don't you get some sleep yourself. You can visit later this evening."

The deep rumble of two old diesel engines came from beneath the wooden deck. The gentle rolling of the worn river tug reflected the slight chop on the Thames. In the pilot house, Bill O'Hanlon sat on a tall stool watching Liam Hennessy on the helm as they moved down river from Exeter Dock.

"Not much traffic out tonight," Liam observed.

"Just as well," O'Hanlon answered. "We never made this trip, so no one is out here to see us."

"As you say, boss."

"Why am I here?" Kent asked.

Jack had just pulled a black cotton hood off the prisoner's head.

Sitting on a simple chair, Phillip Kent's hands were still shackled behind him. Each leg was also locked to the chair with cuffs. A large leather belt bound him to the vertical back of the chair which sat just inside a side hatch on the main deck of the small tug.

"Because we have decided to solve this problem as simply as we can." Jack threw the hood on a small bench attached to the bulkhead.

Kent looked at the two other men and his face reflected the realization that he was in great danger.

"You can't do this!"

"And why not?"

"I have knowledge you want," he said quickly. "I'll tell you everything about the Soviet network in England." Panic showed in his voice.

"But we agreed not to ask you," Jack said, almost casually.

"What?" Now the panic was clear on Kent's face and in his voice.

"Your Soviet bosses gave us permission to terminate you, as long as we didn't ask any questions." Jack kept his voice very steady and conversational. "We intend to honor their request."

A look of terror came over Kent who started to struggle, but he was securely tied to the chair.

"So you are going to die shortly and no one will ever know what happened to poor Phillip Kent. There are several large weights outside this door and we will drop you into the river to sink to the black bottom. You will die alone, j, just another casualty of the war."

"Jack, please don't do this. I'll cooperate."

"You killed Eva Papenhausen, you son of a bitch. You're getting off easy."

Kent looked at them, knowing there was no escape. He slumped in the chair, his chest now racked with quiet sobs.

Fifteen minutes later the engines slowed briefly then the small tug reversed course back toward the Exeter Dock.

Epilogue

Corry Woods
Kent
November 14, 1945

     Admiral Walter Kaltenbach listened as the wind and rain beat against the window of his office. Enough for today, he told himself, slipping the thick folder into a short two drawer safe and spinning the dial. He stood up and extended his arms over his head, trying to stretch the kinks out of his back. He walked to the corridor, turning out the light and closing the door.

     Knocking on the next office door, he opened it and stuck his head in.

     "Albert, I think it's time we retire to the library."

     In a minute the two men walked together down the hallway stopping at another office door.

     "Gentlemen, the senior military and naval officer present request the pleasure of your company in the library."

     A moment later, Jack and Karl joined them in the hallway.

"I'm guessing were already late," Jack said, grinning at the two older men.

"No doubt. Those other two are incorrigible."

After a short walk, the four men entered the library where a crackling fire burned in the fire place. Sitting at a square table, Dmitri and Willy faced each other on opposite sides of a chess board. Each man had several of his opponent's captured pieces lying on the table in front of him. Beside each, a cut glass tumbler of what appeared to be scotch, sat half empty.

"Who's winning," Jack asked.

Simultaneously, without looking up, Dmitri and Willy both said, "I am."

The Admiral and the General laughed.

Karl handed each of the newcomers a drink.

Jack looked around the room and said, "Gentlemen, to good friends."

They all raised their glasses, the light of the fire reflecting bright patterns on the surrounding bookshelves.

Printed in Great Britain
by Amazon

21365463R00130